SUPERWOMAN

The Queen

Printed in the United States of America

First Edition

ISBN-13: 978-1-7336-4422-8
ISBN-10: 1-7336-4422-X

For information regarding special ordering for bulk purchases, contact:
Queendom Dreams Publishing - www.queendomdreamspublishing.com

Queendom Dreams Publishing

Acknowledgements

As always, I give all honor and thanks unto Jehovah God. For without His grace, no talent that I have been blessed with would come to fruition. I thank Him for the past, present, and the blessings to come.

Thank you to all along my path who have supported me in this journey. For those looking for a list of names this time, no can do. I'd have a whole other book filled with acknowledgements, and I know that's not the book you'd want to read from me. Anyone that's anyone knows who they are and don't need acknowledgment in a book to know how priceless they are in my life because I continually let you know personally.

My readers and fans of The Queen, words will never express the level of gratitude I have for you. Without you, I am just another person writing books. Prayerfully, you will stick with me along my journey and inspire me to want to give you more.

Gotta shout out my Queensbridge family. Family for life.

The Queen

SUPERWOMAN

The Queen

Queendom Dreams Publishing

www.QueendomDreamsPublishing.com

Prologue

Roberts, your lawyer is here. Not that it'll do you any good, since you won't be going to see the judge tonight," Detective Shore yelled into the interrogation room, where I had been handcuffed to the table for what seemed like an eternity.

Detective Shore and his partner, Detective Fox, would take turns badgering me, trying to convince me that running over my husband and his pregnant teenage mistress as they were coming out of the maternity store—while I had my kids with me—was premeditated. I'm guessing they felt the need to make a capital murder case against me, as opposed to letting me get by with a moment of insanity.

See, if Derrick had ever taken time out of his busy schedule to take our two boys to their karate practice and our older daughter to the nail salon she goes to with her best friend, which happens to be in the same strip mall as the maternity store, he would have known to take his home-wrecking whore elsewhere. Instead, I had to spend just about fifteen hours trying to convince some overzealous cops that I had no intentions of committing the heinous act.

I had never been arrested before and only had one speeding ticket in my entire forty years of living, but I've seen enough television shows to know how these cops will try to coerce a confession under duress, and being deprived of sleep for all those hours certainly qualified as duress. Heck, I was almost willing to say anything they wanted in exchange for a ten-minute nap. The whole time

I was there, I was given a single slice of pizza, which was a violation to my diet, one orange soda, a single cup of water, and a two-pack of graham crackers. Since Detective Fox joked about the water coming from the toilet immediately after I drained the last drop, I didn't request another cup.

As delirious as I was, I'm pretty certain I requested an attorney first as I was being arrested almost a whole day earlier, and then at least once per hour. Still, they didn't let up with their interrogation and intimidation tactics. They were determined to make this a slam-dunk case for the D.A., yet I wasn't making it too easy.

I came from a good two-parent home, and my mother and father were hands-on in the lives of me, my sister, Janae, and my brother, Johnny Jr. I was brought up in church and had strong family values instilled in me from early on. I completed my bachelor's and master's degree in finance within four years, and I married after starting my career and before becoming pregnant with my first child, just as my mother had done. My parents had been married almost forty-five years, and I had hoped to follow in their footsteps.

Derrick got a job as Dean of Business at the university, and we moved three hours away from Brentwood about a year earlier. Despite the distance, we still made it a point to meet up at my parents' home every fourth Sunday for church and dinner.

Thankfully, I was self-employed and didn't have to up and quit my job or sacrifice time with our three beautiful children. Living in the Memphis area definitely provided more bang for the buck when it came to housing options, compared to the million-dollar homes in Brentwood. We were able to secure an exquisite 5,500-square-foot home in an upscale Collierville neighborhood. Our sons, seven-year-old Bryce and nine-year-old Byron, attended one of the best private schools in the state, while Julie, our fifteen-year-old daughter, attended the School of Music and Arts.

Now, I was thinking this little legal hiccup may present a bit of a problem for Julie's upcoming mega-sweet-sixteen we'd been planning for over a year. It was definitely supposed to be a 'spare no expense' occasion for our firstborn. Derrick had my brother, also known as JJ, hire a few celebrity performers and some dancers, and a BMW X3 was to be delivered to the club we rented for the festivities.

I was the first to give our parents grandchildren, which meant that there was nothing Julie couldn't have. Unfortunately, she'd never let Bryce and Byron forget it. As popular as she was, she insisted on befriending Sandy, who was the biggest gossiper and liar in the school. Worse, Little Miss Gossip was in the car recording while I repeatedly ran Derrick and his teen fling over.

It's not like I didn't know of Derrick's many indiscretions, but something came over me when Sandy yelled out, "Oh my goodness, Julie! Isn't that your dad over there kissing that girl, Brittany? Eew! And she's pregnant!"

All of our eyes shifted to the direction Sandy was pointing, just in time to see my forty-eight-year-old husband holding bags from the maternity store and hugging the eighteen-year-old, apple bottom, pregnant girl from behind as he nuzzled at her neck. They had no shame, nor did they seem to be the least bit concerned with discretion.

I felt my heart swell with greater grief when I noticed the sparkle from Brittany's manicured left ring finger the moment that Sandy said, "Oh man, and check out that huge rock she's sporting." It was clear to see since her hand was holding his left cheek as they stood there like the Couple of the Year.

"MOM!" Julie yelled at me, as if *I* created the embarrassment her father was causing. "Do something! Do you know how embarrassing this is? People are going to clown me! Aren't you going to say something?" she cried.

"Ooh, Daddy's cheating on Mommy!" Byron yelled out, almost giggling.

"WORLDSTAR!" Sandy yelled, as she held up her phone to record the scene, seemingly amused by our grief.

The yelling inside the car and the music that blared from the speakers suddenly seemed to fade away as Derrick and Brittany made their way off of the curb toward his parked Mercedes SLS, which he couldn't live without and which cost almost as much as our home. I watched hypnotized as they frolicked in the parking lot against the passenger door in broad daylight, after throwing the bags in the back seat. I don't know what came over me, but my foot left the brake and floored the accelerator of my 4Runner until the pair was pinned between my grill and his car.

But I couldn't stop there. Although I don't remember it, I supposedly kept reversing and hitting them again and again. Eventually, I was out of my truck and finishing off Brittany and her illegitimate child with my pretty pink Kahr P380 until there were no more bullets. After I snatched the diamond ring my money paid for off her finger, I went on to beat her face up until the cops pulled me off of her corpse. It's a wonder that I wasn't shot to death by the police.

It might seem like the perfect case for a temporary insanity plea. However, it may not be so clear-cut once the detectives really start investigating.

Chapter 1

anelle! Where's my gray and blue tie?" I heard Derrick yell from the top of the stairs.

I had literally just made it in the door from picking my sons up from their music lessons (Bryce on the violin and Byron on the drums). The boys ran in behind me, loudly complaining about how hungry they were because their last meal was lunch at school, and we were just getting in.

Derrick insisted our children took music lessons and perfect some of the tunes of his favorite jazz artists. To be that good, they had to get an early start. That's all fine and well, but for the past ten years, it has been only me taking our children for their lessons, beginning with Julie on the piano at the age of five and her saxophone lessons, which began when she was eight. See, while I did all the hard work of getting them equipped with the skills, Derrick had the easy part, which was attending the recitals. He'd never tell the children about whatever criticisms he had, but he would scold me for their subpar performances and insist that I be firm with the music instructors earning their pay. The crazy thing is, the teachers thought my husband was the kindest, most respectful human being on the planet. Meanwhile, I was the one who got involved in the heated debates and sometimes outright disrespect when I had to convey Derrick's messages about their inadequate teaching.

But when we weren't running the kids to music lessons, it was Julie's cheerleading and dance lessons, as well as her vocal coaching. Oh! Did I mistakenly say "we?" I meant to say, when I—when I wasn't running the kids in addition to everything else. Each of them had private tutors. I took them to that. The boys went to karate and Julie went until she turned fourteen, and I had to take them for that. Seasonally, I took the boys to baseball and basketball practice, while their dad only showed up for the games like Father of the Year, making himself a hero in their eyes.

With Julie turning sweet sixteen in less than a year, I now had to be the Executive Event Planner along with Master of Budgets to keep up with the expense. To Julie's face, Derrick would say, "Whatever my baby girl wants, my baby girl gets. Let's spare no expense to give my baby what she wants." Behind closed doors, he was telling me how much I had to work with and create miracles with. Thankfully, my parents were helping with the costs, but nothing more. Although my brother, JJ, offered to help find some entertainment for the grand occasion, he was certain to let us know the approximate costs.

My day began at 5:30 each morning and went nonstop from there. Prior to my experiencing irregularities in my monthly cycle (almost continuous bleeding), my mornings began at 4:30 with me being sexually available for my husband. I'd then have to get up and get everyone together while he napped until 6:15.

I used to try waiting up for him to come to bed at night, but that became a lost battle almost seven years ago. Derrick had this thing of staying up late, working on papers, watching television, or just "thinking." If he ever was in bed before me, that was either my cue to come to bed or it meant he was not feeling well, which also meant to come keep him company until he fell asleep. If I went off to take care of other tasks while he was asleep, he'd call for me each time he'd awaken. Of course, most times I'd end up sick as a result, and then he'd find a different room to sleep in, because he wouldn't want to get "re-infected" with my germs. When the kids got sick, he would quarantine himself in another room.

After seventeen years of Derrick, trust me, our love life fit right in with all of my other chores. To be quite honest, our relationship became so dysfunctional, it's a wonder we were still married. Don't get me wrong, I loved my husband very much and couldn't imagine my life without him, but at times, he made me feel invisible—almost irrelevant.

We had started this thing called "Date Night," a few months earlier to rekindle a fire in our marriage, and even that became chore-like. Looking at Derrick, pretty much dressed and standing over the rail looking down on me like he was a dictator and I was his peasant, made me think that he was conveniently about to skip our date night that night, as he had done for the past three weeks. Without letting me know.

"Hey Daddy!" Julie said, looking up with such adoration for her father.

Derrick's icy cold glare toward me was replaced with a warm smile as Julie walked in shortly after me. "There's my baby girl. I thought I was going to have to run off to this dinner meeting without getting to see my precious queen."

OUCH! That sucks! I used to be his queen and Julie was always his precious princess. Since I hadn't heard him refer to me as his queen in at least a month, maybe I was demoted and didn't get the memo. After all, what castle has room for more than one queen? And I guess that answered my date night question. Some advance notice would have been nice—AGAIN. It wasn't like I hadn't said as much after the first and second times he bailed.

As Julie ran up the stairs to receive the hug her father held open arms for, I asked, "Oh, no date night tonight?"

"The babysitter left a voicemail saying her father was in a car accident and she couldn't make it. Once I heard the message, I decided to take the business dinner I put off because I thought you and I were going out."

"Well, how about I go with you to the dinner? I'm sure Julie could manage for an hour or two," I said, almost to irk him as much as I was annoyed by his foolish answer. I really was concerned about our babysitter, Kathy, but I couldn't pass up this golden opportunity to get up under his skin.

"That's right, Daddy, I can watch the brats for a little while. You and Mom need to go out together without pesky kids tagging along all the time. I'm fifteen years old," Julie plead on my behalf—for a change.

I wouldn't have been surprised if she, too, had a hidden agenda.

I felt the dagger from the look he shot in my direction, but he smiled and said, "Next time. I would have preferred to give the others notice that I was not coming alone. You know I don't like inconsiderate people, so I can't be inconsiderate to others . . ."

"Except for your wife," I said, pouting. I wasn't hurt about not going, but I was definitely hurt by his thinking it was okay to be inconsiderate to me but not to others.

"Janelle!" he said firmly, as if that were my cue to be quiet, "Could you tell me where my gray and blue tie is at? I really must get going."

"Daddy, are you going to make it to our talent competition on Saturday? Please make it. I am so excited about it. I heard there are supposed to be real people from record companies and different dance companies from around the world," Julie asked, as she made her way to her room.

"Wow! Around the world, huh?" Derrick chuckled. "Wouldn't miss it for the world. We're going to get there early to get a good seat and cheer you on."

What that meant was, I will get there early with the rest of the family and he'll send me text messages to figure out how much time he has to make an entrance without Julie realizing he is missing. Then he'll show up with balloons and flowers, and she won't even care that he was late.

He continued. "If your Uncle JJ makes it, then maybe he could help you make some good connections." He redirected his attention to me. "Janelle, give JJ a call for me and ask him if he could help our baby girl make some connections at the competition."

"Yessa, Massa. Would ya likes me ta do anything else, Massa?" I asked as I made my way up to the bedroom to find the tie he needed to forsake our date in. "You know I aims to please my Massa."

"MOM!" Julie turned and shouted at me. "Why are you being so mean? It's not like Daddy's being unreasonable."

"I believe you were heading to your room, so keep heading there without the commentary," I said to her.

She rolled her eyes and went on into her room, slamming her door.

Derrick followed me into his closet in the bedroom. "Are you jealous of your own daughter? I mean, was that behavior really called for, Janelle?"

I spun around, disbelieving the words I just heard. I opened my mouth to speak, but no words came out. Instead, I shook my head and threw up a hand as a warning for Derrick to back off. I was already angry about him breaking our date, and his giving me tasks on top of tasks was fanning the flames. I was about to open his drawer where he kept certain ties, but then thought against it and left from his closet.

"Where are you going? I need my tie, so I can hurry."

"Find it yourself. I have to call my brother and convince him to come up from Atlanta for Julie's school talent show so you won't think I'm jealous. Oh, no, don't want to upset Julie by being so mean and unreasonable."

"Janelle! Stop being so childish. I have to hurry to dinner," he said, following me out of the bedroom into the hall as he watched me go back down the stairs.

"Speaking of dinner, I have two boys waiting for some. I'm going to go fix it for them. Make sure you say goodnight to them before you go," I said with strain in my voice.

Truth is, I wanted to cry. It wasn't like I didn't know my husband was cheating on me, but I'd never question him about it for fear of him getting angry and leaving our marriage. I'm also certain he was full of it when he said our babysitter's father was in some accident, because I just saw her mother walking into the Chinese restaurant as I drove past it. I'm sure Derrick called Kathy and told her not to come. She was a student at the university, so she would have simply gone to his office, but she never calls the house phone.

I believe the infidelity began when we moved to Memphis and Derrick started working at the university. He worked at the University of Nashville as a Dean also, but the job was hardly as demanding as his current job. Derrick never had a problem taking me to business dinners in Nashville or during our first two months in Memphis, but then it became one. I was suddenly forbidden to call him while he was 'working' because according to him, it was a sign of insecurity, which he would never tolerate. His "business" dinners had him coming home after midnight. Whenever I was with him for a business dinner, we'd be in before ten at night. Since his position in Memphis, he works ridiculously late hours on the nights he doesn't have business dinners.

Sometimes I felt Derrick remained married to me just to keep his friendship with my disloyal brother. Sadly, I believe JJ fed other women to my husband. I know for a fact that JJ was always pulling Derrick aside to show him the smut videos on Facebook or Instagram, and he was always inviting Derrick to Atlanta to go to the strip clubs. Where's the family loyalty?

As I stood in the kitchen making turkey tacos for the kids and helping the boys with their homework, in walked Daddy of the Year looking chipper. He even gave me a big hug from behind as he kissed me in his favorite spot—my neck, underneath my ear.

I won't lie, it turned me on, but I knew better than to anticipate sex anymore. My feelings were crushed way too many times. I guess he was putting on a show for our sons, because the security of having a loving mom and dad was evident in their eyes.

"Don't you have the best mom in the whole wide world?" he asked them, and they anxiously agreed. "Your dad has to go out for a business meeting, so you might be asleep before I make it back in tonight, but after you eat and finish your homework, maybe you all can pop some popcorn and watch a movie with your mom. She was really looking forward to our date tonight, but Kathy couldn't make it because she had to study for her midterms."

I know this was that moment I should have stopped him and called him on his lie, but it would be pointless. He would swear he never made the previous comment, thus a waste of my time. And how dare he get these kids all excited about watching a movie with me, when I mentally planned on having me a Calgon night after the boys went to bed? Jerk!

He continued. "And if you don't mind, I'd like for you guys to tell me what it was all about tomorrow evening when you get in."

Byron and Bryce jumped off of their stools, celebrating as if they had just won some grand prize. They were betting who would tell the movie better. Little did they know, neither would tell it because I had no intention of watching anything. I was in possession of a great book I planned on digging into. I'd only been able to read chapter one.

Derrick dug into his briefcase, "You know what? I forgot I had this for my little guys." He pulled out a DVD of the latest Avengers movie.

"OH MY GOSH!" Bryce yelled with tears in his eyes. "Daddy, you're the best daddy ever!" he said, hugging Derrick around his hips.

After his play-fainting episode, Byron got up from the floor to also run and hug Derrick. "No, you're the *bestest-bestest* dad in the whole wide world, out of this universe, *bestest.*"

I wanted to puke.

I was so sick of the gushing over "King Derrick" while mom couldn't do anything good enough. Not that I felt we were in some type of competition, but it would have been nice to feel appreciated sometimes.

"Don't forget to have your mom make popcorn so you can eat while you watch," he told the boys while trying to pry himself free from their holds.

"Who's making popcorn and watching what?" Julie asked, as she came into the kitchen and pulled open the refrigerator.

"Daddy got us *The Avengers* to watch in the theater room. He told Mom to fix us some popcorn to watch it," Byron yelled with excitement.

"Oh cool, something to keep you brats busy while I work on my blog."

"Julie, I want all of you to watch together. I'm sure your mom could use the company."

"Derrick, I was planning on reading tonight. I've been trying to read the same book for almost a week now and only made it through chapter one."

"That's usually an indication that the book is no good. If the book was good, you wouldn't be able to put it down," Derrick rebutted.

I looked at him as if he were stupid. "Lack of time would be another indication."

"Another indication that it's a bad book?" Julie questioned.

"No, I would have already finished reading my book if I had the time."

"Well, you read with the boys each night before bed. That should satisfy your craving," Derrick said with a shrug.

I smiled through gritted teeth to prevent telling him to take the night off from one of his whores to watch movies and read with the boys.

"Okay, Daddy's gotta run now. Be sure to help your mom clean up the theater room when you're done with the movie," he said as he kissed each of our children on their foreheads.

After dinner, we watched Avengers with popcorn, which I had to clean up by myself as the boys got their baths. After that, I read them to sleep.

Oh, I hated him!

Chapter 2

anelle, wake up."

I rolled over after the gentle tug from Derrick. I swear it seemed as if I just put my head on the pillow. Being no light was permeating my eyelids, I guessed it was safe to assume that the sun had yet to rise.

"Come on, Jan, we're going to be late for church. It's almost 5:30. Get up!"

This coming from a man still lying in bed. Although service didn't begin until 9:45, somehow, we managed to be late just about every Sunday. And before you're ready to hand my darling husband a Saint of the Year award for trying to be on time, he liked to rush to get a certain seat up front so he could be seen by the disrespectful hussies who liked to shamelessly flirt with him. Then he'd act like he was dedicated to our family. I've come to realize that his words only caused them to try harder.

"I don't want to go today. I'm exhausted. I just made it to bed at 1:45," I mumbled into my pillow.

He pulled the pillow from under my head. "Whose fault is that? You stay up at night trying to read those smut-filled books. What do you expect?"

I wished I could deck him good, just once. That was so disrespectful.

"Give me my pillow! I'm not going!" I sat up and firmly asserted.

"I am the man and the head of this household, and I said get up, because you ARE going to church this and every other Sunday. You will not disrespect me or this household. Furthermore, I have little appreciation of my wife reading those sex books. You're not some little teenager. Then you wonder why you're always so horny. Stop reading those types of books!"

"Okay, King Derrick, who somehow now thinks he's my father. If I'm horny, it's because my husband is incapable of satisfying me with a twice-a-month romp in the hay—sometimes less than that. And how exactly did you conclude that my book is a sex book from looking at the cover? There's nothing sexual on the cover."

"One of my students read *Tapioca Pudding Next Door* and told me the disgusting details."

"You're a Dean of Business. WHY would your students feel comfortable having discussions with you about a sex book?" I asked, snatching my pillow from him and lying back down. I didn't even expect a response, since I knew he just got backed into a corner.

"Janelle, it's 5:30, could you get up and get breakfast started? I'd really like to get to church on time this morning. You know it's difficult getting the boys moving," he said, switching his entire demeanor. He cuddled up behind me as if he were actually going to grace my vagina with his royal rod.

THAT caused me to shoot up from the bed. I was so tired of him acting like he was going to make love to me, when in fact he had no intention.

When he skipped our date night to go on his "business" dinner a few nights earlier, he came in sometime after one in the morning. I could smell the alcohol on his breath as he kissed all around my neck and rubbed my breast while he humped on me from behind. His hand roamed my body, causing all kinds of excitement. I turned my head toward him, thinking he would kiss me as he prepared for the sex act, but then he said, "Oh, I'm sorry to bother you. I don't know what came over me." He rolled over, facing the other direction. Now how was I supposed to take that? Minutes later, he was snoring while I spent the rest of my night awake, hot and bothered.

As much as I hate to admit it, he was absolutely correct when he said my book was causing me to be horny. I am not one for porn, but reading that book was like watching pornography with a plot: a rare treat.

"Wow! I can't hold my wife anymore? You saving yourself for someone?"

I spun around, shocked by his accusation. "You of all people can't be serious, could you?"

"What exactly are you implying?" he asked as he sat up on the bed.

I couldn't chance it. I could not risk my husband leaving me and breaking up our family all because of pure suspicions. I honestly didn't have any concrete proof of Derrick's infidelity, but his late nights out and him not making love to me just seemed pretty darn compelling. He barely made it in time for Julie's talent competition last night, talking about he had some work to finish up. I always wondered what I'd do if I ever knew for certain.

"I'm sorry. I'm just a little frustrated these days," I humbly backpedaled.

"Yeah, you need to watch that tone, because I really could not tolerate living in a contentious home with a disrespectful wife, and our children don't need that nonsense in their lives."

"You're right. I'm sorry." I turned away from him so he wouldn't see me rolling my eyes. He could accuse me of saving myself for someone, but if I turned it back on him, I was responsible for busting up the family? The nerve.

"Good! Now, you can fix me some blueberry pancakes to make me feel better," he said with a huge grin.

"I don't want us to be late for church this morning," I said with my subtle sarcasm. "We're going to have to eat Cheerios, bananas, and juice."

"Absolutely not! We need some kind of meat protein."

"Sorry, we don't have time," I said as I rushed off to the bathroom to turn on the shower so I wouldn't have to hear his protest. I could still hear him talking even after I closed the door, but the sound of the running water drowned out his noise.

"I would hate for our family to be broken up over something like pancakes or me making really simple requests of my wife," Derrick said, startling me while I washed my body. He stood outside the shower with his arms folded, seemingly enjoying my discomfort. I still had suds on me and felt uneasy with his presence and his talk of breaking up our family.

He continued. "There are way too many women out here hoping for an opportunity to have the prize you already have. I doubt that they would give me such grief over some pancakes. What do you think? Do you think I should leave you to go find out?"

The tears streamed down my face as he posed the threat he had issued so many times in the past to get me to do what he wanted. He knew that was my weak spot. I wanted to tell him to go, but I didn't dare break our family cycle of marriages—only death was supposed to do us part. I could hear my mother chastising me. Even worse would be my sister, Janae, who swore my marriage wouldn't last from the time I announced my engagement. Each time I saw her, she was always saying, "It won't be much longer now. You just mark my words." If she only knew half the hell I had to put up with from Derrick, just to prove her wrong.

I contracted a venereal disease almost two years earlier, and my husband insisted that I had to get it from a dirty toilet seat, because *he said* all of his tests came back negative. I kept that to myself. Funny thing, he never accused me of getting it from another man. Nonetheless, he didn't touch me for a whole month—maybe longer—but he was never angry about my having Chlamydia. Woo-hoo! Lucky me to have such an understanding husband. Note my sarcasm.

Derrick stared me down, seriously anticipating a response about some doggone pancakes. I finally conceded.

"Fine, I'll make pancakes! Now can I finish washing in peace?"

His icy glare quickly melted, and his smile showed triumph before looking over my body like I was a slave for a prostitute ring.

"You on your period?" he asked, rubbing the back of my neck. "You mind if I join you?"

Oh my lord! I wanted to scream. There was no right answer to give him. If I lied and said I was bleeding, he'd want me to go down on him. If I said I was not, he'd want me to bend over and touch my toes while he slammed me from behind. If I refused him, he'd find many ways to punish me.

"Derrick, if you get in this shower, we won't have time for pancakes. So, you're going to have to choose."

He was already peeling off his underwear before I could finish my sentence. "I'm sure you can get it done," he persisted as he stepped into the shower.

After the shower, I had to fight to get the boys up while Derrick woke Julie up. I had to make pancakes before getting myself ready for church.

Chapter 3

Aw, man! Someone is in our seat. I told you to get up this morning," Derrick said as we walked into the sanctuary at 9:44.

No, Derrick, you should have stayed out of my shower and eaten cereal for breakfast. Then you would have made it in time for your seat.

I never quite understood the concept of people who call themselves saints, yet they are willing to fight in the church over a stupid seat. Even worse are the ones who shove for a space closest to the altar when it's time for prayer.

"Why don't you go find a seat?" I suggested. "I think I'm going to go sit with First Lady Hill. I want to ask her about letting her granddaughter babysit for us sometimes when Kathy is unavailable."

"Which granddaughter? Why can't you wait until after service? My wife should be seated with me. You wouldn't want to give people the impression that we have problems in our marriage, do you?"

Good thing he was behind me and couldn't see me roll my eyes. He was a real piece of work. Such a hypocrite!

"Fine. Where are we sitting?" I impatiently asked. He scanned the sanctuary, as if looking for someone in particular.

"Come, let's sit. It's time for altar prayer." He took me by the hand and led me toward the front of the church and we had to squeeze into the same row with a few of his fan club members. They had the nerve to be all giddy, as if some rock star just slid into their row. I'm not sure why Julie gets to sit up in the balcony with her friends and I can't sit with our first lady, especially when there was room for us to both sit there.

As we squeezed by the four women with ease, I turned back just in time to see one of them rub her breasts against my husband's back as he passed by, while another reached her hand over to grope his butt.

As he wore a huge welcoming smile on his face, he said, "Ladies, I have a wife whom I love very much," he said in a weak attempt to chastise them. One of the women rolled her eyes at me as the others giggled. At the same moment, altar prayer was called, and Derrick wanted us to squeeze past the hoochies to get to the altar. Since they wanted to stay behind, I made it a point to let my heel crush into the foot of the one who rolled her eyes at me, and I didn't bother to apologize.

"Now I know you know you stepped on my foot," she yelled out loudly to cause a scene. I didn't bother to look back and she yelled out a string of cuss words along with a threat of what would happen when I returned from the altar.

"Carmen! We're in church! Chill!" one of her friends scolded.

"Well, I'll see her after church and take her man in the process," Carmen snapped back.

Derrick turned toward the women and then looked at me, pulling my hand as if I were some disobedient child. "Did you do something to Sister Carmen?"

Sister Carmen?! Isn't that supposed to be a title reserved for those who act sisterly? And how does he know their names? I don't even know them.

"What?" I innocently asked. "I've been holding your hand the entire time."

"Oh, okay. She must be talking to someone else. Her behavior is really out of order."

"I agree."

We pressed our way to the altar to be prayed over for what seemed like a good twenty minutes, and then Minister Hill, the Pastor and First Lady's son, decided he wanted to add to the prayer. I guess he was afraid that the sins of

Carmen would cause us all to go to hell, because the next ten minutes of prayer seemed to be directly tied to her ungodly behavior in the sanctuary.

I know one thing—my feet were killing me by the time prayer was done. I needed prayer for my feet. Surprisingly, when we returned to our seats, there were no disturbances. Must have been the prayer.

After service, the gracious heathens wanted to hug me and my husband. Of course, Carmen didn't hug me in the same manner as she hugged Derrick, but she definitely played nice.

"Come on, honey. We don't want to miss First Lady," I said to pry my husband out of the clutches of the Jezebels.

"Okay, babe," he said to me like a loving husband.

"Stop by the restaurant this week, Brother Derrick. Your catfish dinner will be on me," Carmen said, looking at me with a wicked smile.

"Oh, that sounds lovely. Thank you so much," I answered before he could. I knew the invitation was supposed to be a jab at me, but I wouldn't give her the satisfaction. "Do you mind if we bring the kids also? They really love catfish. They're going to be so excited when we tell them. Right, honey?"

It was clear that Carmen and crew were thrown off their game. Derrick had a cheesy smile on his face as he looked at Carmen for a response.

"Uh . . . Oh . . ." she said.

"I believe the invitation was just for Derrick," one of her annoyed friends instigated.

"Oh. Well, in that case, I'll have to decline. That would be quite disrespectful to my wife and my family."

I actually liked Derrick in that moment. He could be a jerk, but in moments like that he reminded me of why I stayed.

"Well, I just figured because you come in a couple of times a week. I certainly wasn't attempting to be disrespectful," she said looking pitiful.

Derrick's expression suddenly switched to BUSTED!

And then it was moments like that when I couldn't stand his raggedy, cheating behind.

"Oh. Well, I'll see. It always depends on if my busy schedule will permit it. But I definitely have to bring my family by the restaurant. After my mother and wife, you cook a mean catfish."

Ha! Take that, you hussy! I thought.

The look on her disoriented face was priceless.

"Come on, Carmen, we have to get going," one of the women said, and the others agreed.

"I guess I'm going to have to work harder to reach that number-one spot."

"Never!" I said with a smile, and then Derrick placed his arm around my waist, letting me know to keep quiet.

The instigator decided to chime in again, further annoyed by the turn of events. "I'm sure a cook-off between you two would determine who's really number one."

"Right!" another said. They high-fived like we were at a ball field instead of church.

"Actually, my mother holds the number-one slot, so no one will ever trump that."

"Well, what about between these two?" one friend asked.

"Sorry, I have a husband, family, and business to take care of. I don't have time for trivial matters. It's not like I have anything to prove." I chuckled to make them feel small.

"Sister Janelle." Everyone came to attention as the tall, stout seventy-one-year-old first lady walked up with her cane.

"Mother Hill, how are you?" I said, turning to give her a hug.

The other women seemed bothered that our first lady knew my name. "Mother Hill! You're looking beautiful as always"

Suddenly, I had an Amen choir coming from the hussy section. Mother Hill wasn't one to act phony, and if she didn't like you, you wouldn't have to wonder much. She took my hand and turned to walk away. Derrick stood as if he didn't know whether to follow us or to stay. I reached for his hand to let him know to come along.

When we made it to another part of the sanctuary, she turned to us and said, "I didn't wan' nothin', chile. I just know trouble when I sees it, and dem girls ain't nothin' but."

I smiled and gave her another hug. I felt special.

"Brother Roberts, dem girls bad news. Dey'd have yo marriage a mess if ya let 'em in," she said, taking Derrick's hand.

He smiled uncomfortably. "Yes, ma'am. I agree. That's why I let them know I have a lovely wife every time I see them."

"So!" she snapped. "Dey don' care nothin' 'bout no wife. Dats when dey try harda. You gotta pra'tect ya family. It's all you have sometime."

"Absolutely." He smiled.

"Give dem babies a kiss fo' me," she said, holding onto both of our hands.

"We most certainly will," I told her. "Oh, Mother Hill, we were wondering if Brittany could babysit for us sometime when our other babysitter is unavailable. Do you think that would be fine?"

"She ain't doin' much dese days. She oughta be o'er at the university with Brother Roberts. Maybe you can talk some sense in dat girl," Mother Hill said, taking a seat on one of the pews.

"Do you think she might still be grieving the loss of your daughter? That has to be very difficult."

"Dat been fo' years now. You can ask her. I'm sho she be a'ight with it."

"Great! I'll give her a call this week," I said.

"And I'll have a chat with her about getting in school soon," Derrick added.

"Good. Good!"

"Well, we better get going. People are starting to come in for the next service, and we have to ride all the way to Nashville for dinner at my parents' home."

I bent to kiss Mother Hill on her cheek while Derrick bent to kiss her other cheek.

"That would be so wonderful if you could help Brittany get in school," I said when we walked out of the church. "I could only imagine how tragic it must be for her, having her mom murdered by her father. And from what I've heard, he was messing with Brittany."

"Wow! That's just horrible. How could a grown man mess with a child like that? Isn't she just now eighteen? Was that her biological father?"

"I don't know, but it shouldn't matter. I guess guys look at the booty she has on her and just lose their ever-loving mind. I've even seen some of the men here in the church behaving so disrespectful toward her, right under Pastor's nose."

Derrick shook his head. "I definitely need to keep a close eye on Julie. Speaking of which, where is she?"

"She and Sandy probably went over to the other building with the Children's Church. I don't see them at the car."

"Who is Sandy? Do I know her? What's her story?"

This was one of those times when I wanted to really tell him about himself. The reason he didn't know anyone was because he was never around. That girl was almost a permanent fixture in our household.

"Sandy lives next door. That's Dave and Angela's youngest daughter. She's a little messy one. I'm not too thrilled about her, but Julie acts like she can't breathe without a day of Sandy in her life."

"What kind of grades does she get? Is she into boys?"

He would have had a heart attack—and it would be my fault—if I told him Julie talked nonstop about boys. She talked about them so much that I considered taking her for some form of birth control, but I knew Derrick would die if he caught wind.

"Sandy gets really good grades. She and Julie study together."

"That's my princess. She makes me so proud," he said, gushing with pride as we walked into the other building to pick up the kids.

"By the way, thank you for the kind words about my catfish. It meant a lot to me," I said, snuggling up on his arm. In that moment, I felt glad to be Derrick Roberts' wife.

Just that moment.

Derrick laughed so hard tears spilled of his eyes. "Are you kidding? Why do you think I eat there twice a week? Carmen's catfish would dance circles around yours, but I would never tell her that. Just like Mother Hill said, those women are only looking to tear our family apart. I would never let that happen. Divorce costs way too much and is way too messy, and it would be extremely hard on our children, so we owe it to them to do all we can to block the infiltrators."

WOW! Talk about a dagger right in the throat. I had to fight the tears as Byron and Bryce approached us. I knew Derrick could be callous at times, but that totally topped every other occasion. So he basically just told me he was only staying married to me because of our children. I was supposed to allow him to treat me like dog doo until the children were grown?

Oh, I hated him!

Chapter 4

Momma Joyce, you have certainly outdone yourself today. Those stewed oxtails just melted in my mouth," Derrick said to my mother, patting his stomach at the table during our monthly family gathering a couple of weeks after the catfish debacle.

"The cornbread was delicioso too," Bryce added.

"It was the best cornbread ever," Byron contributed.

Everyone laughed at their continual competitiveness.

"Momma Erma, your fried cabbage was exceptionally good," I said to my mother-in-law.

She smiled. "Thank you, my sweet."

There were times I thought of leaving Derrick, but the thought of losing my mother- and father-in-law was quite unsettling to me. Unlike many, I loved my in-laws —more than I loved my husband. Even my two sisters-in-law were wonderful. Definitely better than my own sister.

"Well, ain't nobody talk about how good service was this morning," my dad grumbled. "People always talking about what's good to their belly, but never what's good to their soul."

My father-in-law pounded his hand on the table, "Amen, Brother John! This younger generation don't be thinking."

"No, siree! They living on the prayers of our grandmothers," my dad responded.

"You know, the word says that man ain't supposed to be worrying over no food, because they supposed to be fishermen of souls. And fire and brimstone will rain down upon all these folk who don't have their lanterns prepared with oil for the coming of the Lord."

"Yes! Yes, sir! Preach it, Brother Paul!" my dad encouraged my father-in-law. "You ain't telling no lie! And the scriptures say that all these youngins running around getting their bodies marked up with all that ink will be unrecognizable to the Master, and he will cast them into a fiery pit."

Poppa Paul stood, knocking his chair over, banging on the table, saying, "Yes He will!"

Okay, this was my cue to leave from the table. Every fourth Sunday, both of our families got together for church and dinner at my parents' home in Nashville, and each time both of our fathers would make up stuff not found in any version of the bible. Our mothers would start arguing with them, saying they were just making up junk. The quad would go on for hours, with the women pulling out bibles and reading verses, while the men gave their "special" interpretations of the scripture.

Derrick always went off to another part of the house with my brother. They always acted secretive and got quiet if I entered the room.

I loved when Derrick's sister, Denise, came to dinner with her husband, David, and their eight-year-old twin boys. David would go off with JJ and Derrick to their secret place, while I got to spend time with Denise, as opposed to being stuck with my sister Janae. When Derrick's youngest sister, Wanda, came, JJ broke up the guy time to behave like a kid with a crush. He was on his best behavior this time, and not the normal jerk he typically is. Wanda was a long-time model who lived in New York with no kids. She traveled out of the country often, which would be the reason she missed many of our fourth Sunday gatherings. Occasionally, David's parents would come in from North Carolina, as amused spectators of mine and Derrick's parents. They wouldn't partake in biblical debates. A couple of times a year, on a different Sunday, we would all visit David's family in North Carolina, just to be fair.

In one sense, it was a really beautiful thing when we all came together and there would be so many years of strength in marriage. It helped keep me going in my own marriage. However, on the other edge of that sword, was the exceedingly high expectation to stay in my broken marriage and put up with the disrespect. I often thought about how I'd feel if my daughter was in such a marriage. I'd probably advise her to bail, especially if her husband did what Derrick did to me two days following the catfish incident at church.

Derrick came home from wherever he was that evening. I was already in bed, because it was after eleven. He brought this greasy brown bag into the bedroom, waking me from my peaceful sleep so I could taste how good Carmen's catfish was. Because I disagreed with him, he took it upon himself to arrange a catfish cook-off for charity, to be held on the school's campus. When I let him know I would not be competing, he refused to come home that following night. He said he wanted me to see what my life would feel like without him in it. Little did he know, I slept like a baby. I didn't miss him at all until my alarm clock went off and there was no one there to rush me out of the bed when I hit the snooze on the clock. He happened to walk in right at that moment, seeming extra happy. He was so happy, he called off the catfish cook-off.

I also would have told my daughter to leave her husband if he did as Derrick had done a few days after that, telling me how sexy Carmen was and how everything on her body was one-hundred percent natural. He suggested that I become friends with her so I could work out with her to get her body. Of course he brought home some of her fish.

But the worst to date was a few nights later, when he asked if I realized how lucky I was to be married to him. He said if he wasn't married to me, he could see being up inside of Carmen every night. When I began crying from his cruel words, he still tried to justify himself by reminding me that he married me, but a man is always going to look and fantasize. So then he wanted to make love, and he called me Carmen several times during the process. Afterward he told me how much he loved me and that I'd never have to worry about him leaving me—because I let him pretend I was someone else, specifically Carmen.

Janae spied the misery in my face as I tried to clean up the kitchen the next day.

"What's up, Big Sis? Trouble in paradise?"

"Please! You wish. Where's your husband? Oops! I forgot, you don't have one, you bitter old maid," I responded, fighting my tears.

"Hey, hey! Why all the hostility toward me?" she came and wrapped her arms around me and I let the tears flow. "I can look in your face and see you are deeply bothered by something. I don't care how much I pick with you, you are my big sister, and I look up to you and I love you. You don't have to tell me anything going on in your marriage, but I'd highly suggest you speak with someone. You keep trying to hold stuff in, and one day you're liable to snap. I don't want to visit my sister in any prison or mental hospital."

I wanted to talk with someone so bad, but I hardly thought my younger sister was that someone. If I told her I didn't want to be married to Derrick anymore, she would have been elated. I'd never give her such satisfaction.

I stepped away from her embrace, wiping my tears. "Thank you. I needed that. And I'm going to take your advice." I smiled. I felt like a load was lifted from my shoulders.

"So, you *are* having trouble in paradise, huh? Doesn't surprise me. I don't like Derrick. I don't trust him. I don't think you should either. You need to go find you a fling, because I could bet my life that your husband has a few young ones. I'm sure he's changing grades all day long in exchange for sexual favors. You need to get rid of him before he gives you some disease."

Little did she know.

She continued. "And do you see how he is in church? Why must he be hugging all these different women? That's so disrespectful. He stays gone so much, I bet he doesn't even know your children's names."

She was on a roll, and as angry as I was for her butting her nose in my marriage, I bust out laughing. When Janae was over about a month ago, Derrick kept talking about "Brian," and we wondered who he was talking about. Eventually, we realized that he was talking about our son, Byron. Although I hardly found it to be a laughing matter back then, it sounded hilarious coming from Janae.

"You know I'm telling the truth. That's why you're laughing."

"Mind your business!" I continued laughing. "I'm just laughing at you because you really think you know something about my marriage. When are you going to get a husband that we can talk about? I'm starting to wonder if you're gay since we have yet to see you with any guys. I remember a few years ago when you brought 'Loosey-Lucy' home for dinner. She acted like a little puppy dog, following you everywhere."

Janae turned away as if I had hit a nerve. "Trust me, I like men. Lucia is just a friend I met in Brazil. She had never been in the United States, so naturally she would be a little clingy."

"She was beautiful. They say Brazilian women are beautiful, is that true of all of them?"

"Why don't you and your loving husband take a trip there and see for yourself?"

I turned away that time. I didn't dare tell her that Derrick was scheduled to take a so-called business trip to Brazil without me in six weeks. It was supposed to be part of some international student exchange program.

"Are you kidding? Do you know how much a trip like that would cost a family of five? Don't forget, we have Julie's sweet sixteen coming up in about nine months. That thing is going to cost a fortune. And then we have the Disney cruise this summer, remember? We have Byron, Bryce, and Daddy's birthdays, in addition to Mother's Day and Father's Day. Oh, and Mama Erma's birthday is coming as well."

"Funny. No mention of your birthday. Don't you deserve something special? You go overboard for Derrick's birthday."

"That's because I'm the planner. I organize everything."

I laughed, but Janae was not amused.

"Lighten up, Baby Sis. If it'll make you feel better, I'll let my husband take me to the Brazilian Steak House for my birthday."

"You are so pathetic. And if you want to know why I won't get married, it's because I don't want to end up like you—pathetic!! You are so miserable and you have a husband who isn't the slightest bit concerned with making you happy or a priority. Thanks, but no thanks. I'll stay by myself and do as I please, when I please."

I stood at the sink, scrubbing imaginary stains from the roasting pan to keep Janae from seeing my tears forming. This was why I hated being around her. She was so mean—or maybe it was just that the truth hurts. I would hate for my younger sister to be married to a "Derrick."

"Oh, and that Julie—you better get a firm grip on that brat. I'm not sure why you're spending all that money on a birthday party. You and I turned sweet sixteen, and we survived without a $100,000 birthday party. You've been watching too many of those baller sweet-sixteen shows. She is too disrespectful, and as much as you do and give for her, she bosses you around, telling you what she will or won't do. She needs a good old fashion butt-whooping."

"DON'T YOU DARE talk about my children like that. It's one thing for you to talk about my husband, but you absolutely need to back off, speaking negatively about any of my children."

That is where I draw the line. My children are completely off limits, although I agreed. Julie got away with murder because she was Derrick's do-no-wrong child. So many times I wanted to smack her but didn't out of fear of the repercussions. I'd tell her to do something and she'd tell me what she was going to do or not do. I told her she'd have a sleepover at a hotel with a few of her closest friends and somehow that turned into a huge $100,000 affair. I tried to plan mother-daughter dates, and she'd invite her friends, calling me lame. The only time she spent alone was when Derrick ordered her to do so, after I had to involve him. She'd act so ugly and miserable to the point where I would cut our time short. Derrick would take her on a father-daughter date twice a month, and she would actually spent the day getting cute in preparation.

One day she had the audacity to tell Janae that I couldn't stand her because she was nosey and always meddling in everyone's business. I did say that, but to Derrick ONLY. He felt the need to share my feelings about Janae, with Julie, an unruly teenager.

That whole day was a disaster. After Julie said her part, Janae said something about Julie, and Julie told Derrick. Derrick confronted Janae for being out of line, then told her that I said way more than that about her. Janae dealt the final blow, telling Derrick that I wished he'd learn some new skills to please me in the bedroom. He was sooooooo angry that he searched the house for me. He found me in the bathroom and said some very cruel things to me. He didn't bother to ask if I had really said those things to Janae. When he left the bathroom, leaving me to wipe away my tears, Janae found him and told him she had just made it up, because he deserved it for acting like a donkey. She laughed on the outside of the door, while I cried from the emotional pain inflicted upon me.

When I learned that all of my grief was a result of Julie, I wanted her punished, but Derrick wasn't having it. Instead, he rewarded her with a prepaid credit card loaded with $500 to go shopping. That caused me to wonder if the whole situation with Janae was orchestrated. Why else would Julie be armed with the information I only said to Derrick? Although I momentarily hated Janae because of her role, I realized I couldn't stay angry with her and not the others. Particularly, because she was correct about my wishing Derrick improved his bedroom techniques. I just never told anyone. I don't understand how Janae always seemed to know my unspoken thoughts and feelings. Maybe it's a sister thing.

"Maybe I shouldn't say it so harshly, but it makes my blood boil when I see how she acts with you, compared to Derrick. I always wonder when he's going to put her in her place, but he never does. The irony! I bet if you left his butt tomorrow, he wouldn't even fight for custody of her and she would rebel against you. That worries me. It makes me think you're happy trapped in that farce of a marriage."

"Lay off of my marriage, my children, my family, and my life. Let's talk about Janae's wonderful life for a change."

"Sure. What do you want to talk about? My life's an open book. I have nothing to hide. But while we're on the subject, I think you need to hire a private investigator so you can see what your husband is really up to."

"What? Where did that come from? Why would I do something so foolish?"

"There's nothing foolish about it. It's called making informed decisions. If he got home tonight and said, 'Janelle, I want a divorce,' where would that leave you? You need to find out where your money goes outside of the home. You need to find out if he has hidden assets or secret apartments he's taking his students to. You need to be prepared at all times. Never let your guard down. And always make sure you keep a little pocket change on the side that he doesn't know about. You never know when it might come in handy."

"Stop it! You're ridiculous! You watch too much television. I thought we were supposed to be talking about you."

"Did I ever tell you about this guy I ran a background check on? I found out he was locked up twice for missing his child support payments for children he claimed not to have. Yep! He had three different baby mothers and had the nerve to ask me to have his baby so he could spoil him or her." Janae laughed. She laughed really hard. "Then I learned that he had a wife living in Alabama while he mostly stayed in Atlanta. One of his children lived in Mississippi, another in Arkansas, and the third in Florida. Keep in mind, those are just the ones in the court system. There's no telling how many more."

"Are you serious?" I laughed. It felt kind of cool for my sister to share her kooky life for a change.

"Yes, girl! I had this other guy who had some real estate or construction company. Oh, he was living big time. He was so fine and buff. He'd spare no expense to please me. I did a check on him and found out that he owned a business with no business. He was an ex-con with multiple jail terms for selling drugs. When I found out his so-called prosperous company didn't even have a bookkeeper, I knew that was a red flag. He didn't have a single contract."

"Wow! You have had some adventures. We need to talk more."

"Yeah, this is kind of cool talking with my sister for a change. It's just that you always act like your life is so perfect, and you always try to make me feel bad about not being married."

I walked over to the counter stool she was sitting on and took her hands into mine. "I am so sorry for making you feel bad. Sometimes I get so caught up in this whole perfect marriage thing because of our family, that I lose sight of the fact that you might actually be happy."

"I'll admit, sometimes I do wish I was married, but when we get together on fourth Sundays, that desire goes out of the window. I don't want to go through my life pretending to be happy because I'm worried about what other people might think or say. If someone hurts me or makes me cry, I want to be able to walk away without fear of an ugly court battle. I don't want to be tied to someone who treats me bad because of children. So in that sense, I love my freedom."

I didn't know what to say. She made some valid points. She just described my life.

"Come on. Let's go find the guys and see what they're up to," I said after giving my sister a big hug.

And what a big mistake that was . . .

Chapter 5

"Get up! Come eat your breakfast before you're late for school," I yelled, busting into Julie's room.

"What ever happened to knocking first?" she yelled back.

"Raise your voice at me one more time, so I can stop planning that ridiculous sweet sixteen of yours."

"Daddy would never allow that, so I'm not even going to worry about it," she said, rolling over and pulling her covers over her head. "And close my door on your way out."

I left her room. I was angered to tears. It took everything in me not to put my hands on her and drag her from the bed. But I had something even better for her. I went and got a bucket filled with ice and cold water. I quietly went back into her room and simultaneously snatched off the cover and dumped the bucket of water all over her.

She screamed as if someone was murdering her. "What the hell is wrong with you?"

"What did you say to me?" I challenged her to repeat her words. I was so sick of her nonsense and would smack the taste from her mouth if need be.

Derrick came running into Julie's room. "What's going on?"

"Daddy, look what she did to me and my bed. Please say something to this mad woman. She's in here tripping this morning. First she bursts into my room without knocking, then she comes in here yelling like a crazy woman, and now this mess," she said, pointing to her wet pajamas and bed.

I put my hands on my hips, daring Derrick to say a word. "You have something you want to say to me, Derrick?" I looked him directly in his shifting eyes.

"Do what your mother says," he mumbled before walking out to return to the guest bedroom he was banished to last night.

"Daddy!" Julie cried out.

"Hush that noise. I've had enough of the drama, and if you give me any more grief, you will not—repeat, *will not*—have a birthday party."

She cried as if someone just died.

"Shut up! And hurry up so you can get to school."

I was feeling empowered after walking in on Derrick and JJ last night. Even worse, Janae was with me.

"Man, when she spread those legs open, I just had to take a picture. It was beautiful. I was so mad her granddaughter came barging in that office before I got a chance to touch it. I was too busy snapping all these pictures. Isn't she a beauty?" I heard Derrick saying to my brother.

"Give me her number. I'll try her out and tell you all about it."

"I may as well give you her number since I can't do more than look at it. She's in my church and already giving Janelle grief."

"Nah, you need to handle that. I'm not going to have any of these knuckleheads bothering my sister."

"You want her number?"

"You can just send me a copy of those pictures. I might make this my screensaver. These are some good close-ups. Was you smelling her?"

Derrick laughed so hard and then took a long gulp of his drink.

"Was it fresh or did it need one of those girlie washes?" JJ asked.

"No need for any girlie washes," Derrick answered, nodding his head.

"And you were sniffing up between another woman's legs, why?" Janae asked, busting into the room we just stood outside of, spying and listening. She was HOT!

Although I tried to conceal my tears, as I listened to words straight from the horse's mouth, my nose started running. My sniffle was a giveaway to my sister that I was crying, which caused her to bust through the cracked door.

"You are so ugly," she said to Derrick, and then redirected her attention to JJ as he tried to slither away from Janae's wrath. "And where do you think you're going, Mr. Sneaky Man? How could you be so backstabbing to your own sister? If anything, you should be decking this weasel for disrespecting your sister. What kind of big brother are you? You're supposed to be a protector, not encouraging this punk to hurt your sister. How could you be so spineless?"

I debated on telling Janae about the times JJ would try to get Derrick to Atlanta so he could show him all of the strip joints. Instead, I foolishly put myself on the wrong side.

"Janae, that's enough. You've made your point. They know better now. Besides, Derrick's going to delete those pictures from his phone and he's going to stay away from that woman for good. Right, Derrick?"

Before Derrick could answer, Janae did. "Janelle, how could you be so stupid? Of course he's not going to stay away. Right, Derrick?"

"This is a matter between my wife and I, and we will discuss it in private," Derrick answered, putting his arm around my shoulder without any resistance from me.

"Oh, Janelle! You are stupid! You heard with your own ears and you cried. Does that mean nothing to you?"

I shamefully defended my husband. "My husband is correct. We will discuss this in private."

Janae stared at me as if I'd soon let her know I was joking. When I said nothing, she said, "And you wonder why I won't get married. My brother and your husband would be a perfect indication. Wait till I tell Mama how dumb you are. This is ridiculous."

Little did my younger sister know, I learned my passive behavior from our mother. She was the epitome of foolish, but she still had a husband and a good life to show for it. That was what I wanted. I just couldn't stand Derrick always holding it over my head and basically getting away with murder.

However, this time, I wasn't so passive. When we got home, I went into the storage and pulled out two suitcases. The boys wanted to know where I was going and began crying. Derrick came and snatched the suitcases from my hands and tried to make it seem like I was joking. He then told the boys that they needed to behave to keep me from leaving them. They apologized, but Derrick never did. He simply slithered his way to the guest bedroom after the kids went to bed to avoid any conversation.

When I pulled out the suitcases, it was actually for Derrick to get out, but then I had time to sleep on the situation. I remembered Carmen and her friends thinking they could take my husband, and I would not just hand him over to her or them. Also, I wasn't quite ready to admit I had failed in my marriage.

The three nights to follow brought out a version of Derrick I had hardly known. It was as if he finally realized his work hours were from eight to six. He was home for dinner each night. He even helped with the homework. The greatest shock of all was when I awoke to breakfast in bed, prepared by Derrick and Julie. It didn't taste good at all, but I appreciated the thought.

Things began to quickly go south, though. I waited for Derrick to go to sleep and checked his phone to see what other interesting items I could find. This was an act I had never done and had sworn I'd never do.

But you know what they say. Desperate times call for desperate measures.

Chapter 6

Good afternoon. I'm looking for Mr. Barker," I said to the receptionist in the shabby office.

By the way the receptionist sized me up with her eyes, it was apparent that she was more than just his receptionist. I didn't see any ring on her finger, which let me know she was not a wife. She looked quite young and had a bad weave in her head, done up in many colors. The top she wore was just right for a night at the club, but definitely inappropriate for work—unless you're sleeping with the boss.

"What's yo name? You got an appointment, right?"

And obviously lacking education.

"I do not have an appointment. I just wanted to see how this whole thing works, and if Mr. Barker is the man for the job," I answered with a pleasant smile. She didn't feel the need to return the smile. "I mean, if you'd prefer I leave to make an appointment, I can do that."

"Hol' up! Lemme see if he wants ta see ya. What yo name is?" she rudely asked as she stood up.

Aside from cringing from her poor speaking skills, my eyes were instantly traumatized by the spandex miniskirt that exposed her privates as she stood from her seat. She tussled to pull it down, but her ample bottom made it look as if she were wearing her kid sister's skirt.

"My name is Mrs. Roberts," I told her, still trying to remain pleasant, although everything inside of me was warning me to run from the god-awful establishment.

She went into Mr. Barker's office and closed the door behind her. It took her a few minutes, but as she was coming back out, she turned back and said, "Oh, I forgot, there's someone here to see ya. I forget what her name is. She don't got no appointment. You wanna see her?"

"Send her in," I heard him say.

She turned to me and said, "He'll see ya. Ya lucky, 'cause ya 'pose to have a' appointment when ya come 'round her'."

"Thank you, Stacy," he said, obviously annoyed with her behavior. "Please send her in now."

Stacy stepped aside for me to enter and then closed the door once I was inside his office. The overwhelming smell of sex was nauseating to me

"Forgive her. Good help is so hard to find. She's my fourth receptionist in a year. My wife used to be the receptionist, but she has to stay home now that she had the twins." He stood from his seat and his fly was open. He extended a hand to shake mine, but I just looked at it. "I'm sorry, I didn't catch your name," he said.

"I'm Janelle Roberts. I'm sorry about not being able to shake your hand. I've just gotten over a really bad cold, and I wouldn't want you to get sick and make your family sick," I lied.

"Thank you. Yeah, the wife has a hard enough time managing the twins. When they're sick, she really has a difficult time."

I managed to give him one of my phony smiles, but I could have cared less about him or his family, which he obviously had little regard for.

"Could you give me a little of your background, before I decide whether to go forward with this case or not?" I asked.

"Sure can. I can tell you're very educated and make informed decisions. That's really good."

I smiled again. To me, it's called *common sense.*

"My name is Willard Barker. I was a police officer for about ten years before making detective. I was that for another twenty-five years, when I decided to go into business for myself. You know Memphis; it's not like it was when I first became an officer. Much more dangerous these days. I've been a private investigator now for eight years—"

"Will, yo wife's on the phone. She said she wanna talk to ya, now," Stacy said, barging into the office.

"Stacy, please let her know I'm with a client, and don't interrupt us again," he snapped.

She looked at him as if she were ready to read him, and then looked at me, rolling her eyes. "Uhm hmm. Okay," she said, before closing the door.

"Forgive the intrusion. Stacy is my wife's niece, and she's kind of protective when she sees an attractive woman."

Wow! This boundaryless fool was sleeping with his wife's niece, and he had to be at least sixty or so years old. He'd been working between his three positions for a total of forty-three years.

"So, what type of case were you needing help with? I can help you with everything but husband issues."

I was put off by his comment. "And why is that?"

"I know your husband. Derrick Roberts, right?"

Now I was really kicking myself for not running when I first had the mindset to do so. I couldn't believe my lousy luck. My heart was racing. I was afraid of Derrick finding out about my attempt to dig up information I could use to bury him with in court if need be, or at least get him to act right, as he did before he found me going through his phone.

I went through his phone, not sure exactly what I'd find. I definitely wanted to see the photos he showed to my brother. I was hoping he'd have the decency to erase them from his phone. I saw so many photos of naked women in all shades of brown, as well as white. Ironically, there were no pictures of faces. Every last pic was only from the shoulders down.

I started going through his contacts, but my finger accidentally dialed someone listed with the initials "FP." I quickly ended the call when I heard a woman answer, but her calling back was what woke Derrick and caused him to make his way into the bathroom where I was stowed away.

"What the hell are you in here doing!" he yelled with fire in his eyes. He snatched his phone from my trembling hands.

I was terrified and didn't know why. I should have gone ballistic on him for having naked women and numbers for women in his phone.

"I see the trust is now gone from our marriage. Don't think we have much left after that," he said, going back to the guest room with his phone in tow.

I'm not sure why, but I was actually happy that he moved back into our bedroom. After my violation, somehow the tables turned and I lost my little bit of power. You would think I would have the upper hand with what I had found in his phone, but he turned it around on me once again. Now, the last thing I needed was for Derrick to find out about my visit to Willard Barker.

"Oh my goodness! Please do not let him know. He would die if he knew I was here."

I was furious with myself for failing to come back with a lie to save face. Instead, I just handed the jerk the upper hand. Ol' Willard had the nerve to look at me like a pork chop sandwich—with hot sauce. His grin let me know he was not an honorable man. It wouldn't surprise me to learn that he was booted off of the police force, since he never quite said he retired.

"Yeah, I'd hate for him to find out," he implied, as if I was to fill in the blank.

"Yeah, I'd hate for your wife to find out about Stacy also," I shot back to get him to back off.

I looked him dead in his eye as his eyes challenged me without words.

"And what exactly is it that my wife would find out?" he asked, leaning forward in his seat.

I stood from the seat, walked to the door, and turned back. "I guess nothing, as long as my husband has nothing to find out."

"Get out and don't come back!"

"With pleasure!"

Stacy was standing like a pit bull, ready to attack. She forgot to pull her skirt down before she yelled, "Will, what's up?"

"Your skirt is up so high, that your uncle can see your cookies. That's what's up," I said all too cocky. I had to play the tough role, hoping to have some leverage.

"That's Dean Roberts' wife. You know, the one that changed the grade for you a couple of months ago. She must think he's cheating on her, and need some PI services," Willard said to Stacy.

The pair laughed as if some inside joke was told. I ain't gonna lie, I was rattled. I could just imagine what Stacy would do to have a grade changed.

"For the record, I never came to you and said that I believed my husband was cheating on me, so get your facts straight before you tell them. You said you could help with everything but husband issues, and out of curiosity to your statement, I asked why not. Never did I say I was here concerning him."

"But you said you didn't want him to find out you were here, right?"

"That's correct. That would be right before you tried to proposition me for your silence, and I let you know I would never sleep with your old, dirty behind."

Okay, so I ad-libbed a bit, but that was to get Stacy out of alliance with him.

"Ya did what?!" she yelled at him. "See if ya touch it ever again, and if ya try firing me, I'ma tell my aunt, ya dog!"

I winked my eye at him as he stood with his mouth open. "Have a good day now."

I smiled walking out, but inside I was thinking up a good lie for Derrick for when he learned about my visit to Willard Barker, P.I. I thought perhaps if he brought up the subject, I could bring up Stacy's grade change, with a little ad-lib.

I knew one thing for sure. This would be the last time I ever took advice from my younger sister. No more private investigators for me.

Chapter 7

Mom, why does Brittany need to be our babysitter? She doesn't do anything but watch television and talk on the phone when she's here. I especially don't know why she has to spend the night when she babysits. Why can't she go home like Kathy used to do?"

"Julie, please! I don't feel like going through this right now. Your dad feels it's best that she stays in the guest room since she doesn't drive. He doesn't want to have to take her home late, so he said she should stay."

"And what if we had an emergency and needed to get to the hospital or something? Why have a babysitter that can't drive? That's so stupid. And just make sure you remind her that she's only here to babysit Byron and Bryce. I'm too old for a babysitter. I don't know why I can't just watch the brats."

I laughed. "Yeah, right! I guess you forgot about the time you were supposed to keep up with Bryce at the mall while you were with your friends, and you lost him within minutes. No, I don't think so. As for an emergency, you call 9-1-1. Besides, your dad insists there is an adult here with you at all times, so thank him."

Julie stomped her foot. "Aw, come on! Brittany isn't even an adult. She's just a few years older than me, and she's stupid. She's an air head."

"Why don't you like her? I thought you two were cool in church?"

"'Cool in church' does not mean I like her. She told me how small my butt is and said she had way more booty when she was my age."

"Are you jealous?"

"Seriously? Who would be jealous of Brittany? She's all butt and no brains."

"Well, I think she's a sweet, misunderstood young lady who has had a rough life. Could you imagine what it must feel like to lose a parent because of the other parent?"

Julie got sad. "Yeah, that must suck. Okay, I'll cut her some slack."

"Thank you, and watch your language. You know we don't permit those kind of words."

"Dad lets me say 'suck.' He said it's not a big deal."

"I bet, but I said don't say it, and that's that."

She sucked her teeth and stormed out of my bathroom, where I stood fixing my hair and make up for my date night with Derrick.

I was almost ready to give up on thinking we'd ever enjoy these dates, but surprisingly, the past few dates were pretty decent. Not romantic, but they were more like being out with a good friend.

Derrick picked me up as if we were not married and living together. He showed up to the house and rang the bell. I didn't bother going to the door, because I assumed it was Brittany being dropped off.

"Mommy!" Byron called out, giggling. "Somebody's here to see you."

I came down the stairs and Brittany was already inside the house with a big smile, waiting for my reaction, along with the kids.

"Hi, Brittany. When did you get here?"

"Hi, Miss Janelle. I just got here."

"Oh, I thought Derrick was going to pick you up this evening," I said, heading to open the door.

The kids giggled even more.

I opened the door to find Derrick standing there with a dozen roses, and the kids shouted, "Surprise!"

I was so shocked that I almost fainted—not from the shouting, but from the gesture. I couldn't remember the last time I had received flowers from my husband.

"That is so romantic. This is the kind of marriage I want. I want a thoughtful and romantic husband," Brittany said, gushing with joy.

If only she had a real clue. And I was sure once Derrick found out Aunt Flow came to visit today, he was going to be really disappointed if he was trying to make this a fully romantic night. My cycle was so heavy that it took a super tampon combined with an overnight pad to contain it. Needless to mention, the deathly cramps I was fighting through felt like my uterus was collapsing and passing through my vajayjay.

Looking at Derrick standing there smiling and looking exceptionally handsome while holding the flowers made me really regretful about being on my period. This was one of those times I was actually hoping to make love to my husband. I thought perhaps we were really making strides with this date night thing. Since we switched babysitters, Derrick hadn't missed a single date.

When I went outside to his awaiting car, he even opened the door for me, and closed it after I was inside. He took me to dinner at one of my favorite Italian restaurants and then out for dancing at one of the hotels hosting a live band. We were having a really great time until I saw Willard Barker with some young girl. My heart raced as he approached.

"Roberts, how are you? I wasn't sure that was you."

"Hey, Barker! I'm good. You been hitting the gym lately?" Derrick asked.

"Nah, been real busy lately."

"Oh, that's good. This is my wife, Janelle. I don't think you've met her."

Surely at this point, my heartbeat was audible over the loud music. My eyes pleaded with Willard's eyes, hoping he wouldn't say anything.

"Oh, we just met a few weeks ago when she came to my office."

Derrick's smile became frozen. He didn't like being made a fool of. "Wow! Really?" He turned his attention to me and asked, "What was that all about?"

"I was going to have him look into a situation with my sister, but he acted so disrespectful, I never had a chance to discuss the matter. Then he tried to imply that you were sleeping with his wife's niece, who he is also sleeping with, so she could get her grade changed. I believe her name was Stacy."

I managed to get every word out, just as I had practiced since that eventful day in Willard's office.

"Huh?" Derrick asked puzzled. I could tell he wanted to be angry with me, but would deal with me away from Willard.

"Man, that never happened. Ain't nobody say anything about anybody sleeping with anyone," Willard said, growing angrier by the minute.

"How would I know my husband changed Stacy's grade?"

Just as I said that, Willard's young date walked up behind him with a drink in her hand. The way she pressed against his back made it clear to the world that they, too, were intimate.

"What about my sister?" she asked. "I heard you mention Stacy?"

"Wow! Talk about keeping it in the family." I laughed.

Derrick pulled my arm as if to chastise me. "We'll talk later, in private," he said to Willard.

"Definitely! Give me a call some time tomorrow. I should have some time then."

"Wait, I wanna know what she was saying about my sister," the girl said, as Willard tried to rush her away from us.

Now why couldn't he have just kept his big mouth shut? He was way too old to be acting the way he did. Old pervert!

Our night was immediately cut short because Derrick wanted to get to the bottom of my visit to a PI. As soon as we were in the car, the grilling began.

"So first you're going through my phone, and now I find out you're trying to get people to spy on me?"

"Are you serious?" I said, as if I was offended. "I went to see that guy so I could figure out what my sister is up to. I am so tired of her always talking about my life and marriage, and I really don't have a clue about her life. Her whole life is a great big secret."

That was the remainder of the lie I had rehearsed. I knew I had to be convincing when he asked, "Why would you want to spy on Janae? Why can't you just mind your business sometimes?"

"Derrick, it's not you she calls stupid. You have no idea how it feels to be called such by my younger sister all because you had naked women on your phone." I knew that would shut him up.

We rode in silence for a few minutes, and out of nowhere, he announced, "I'm going to sleep in the guest room tonight. I see the picture thing is still an issue for you, and I just don't feel like doing the drama with you tonight."

I was shocked. He was going to punish me because of his wrongdoing. And worse, he didn't even know I was bleeding. I had yet to let him know. "How are you going to sleep in the guest room and Brittany's in there? Are you taking her home tonight?"

"Don't we have another guest room down in the basement?" he snapped.

"Fine! I'm tired of fighting over nothing. Should I bother waking you in the morning? I have to take the kids to all of their activities. We should be home around dinner time."

He softened his tone. He almost seemed happy. "No, I want to sleep in tomorrow. I thought you didn't have anywhere to be until after noon."

"I have to take them for music lessons, karate lessons, basketball practice, nail salon, lunch, and I promised to take the boys to see that new Disney movie. We have to leave by seven-thirty."

"No, I definitely don't want to be disturbed."

"Shoot! I forgot about Brittany. Julie's friend is supposed to go with us. It's already tight in my truck, and I really don't have time to transport her in the morning. Maybe you could just take her home tonight."

"She's probably already sleeping. If the kids have a full Saturday like that, surely they're all asleep by now. I'll just drive her home when I get up or I could leave money for a taxi for her."

I wasn't sure why I got an unsettling feeling down in my gut.

"Maybe I could take her home at six and come back for the kids," I suggested.

"That's ridiculous. Who's supposed to get the kids up and ready? Who's supposed to fix breakfast? And you'd have to wake her at five or so to leave by six. She's about forty-five minutes in the opposite direction from where you have to go. Are you sure that's what you want to do?"

"It's not forty-five minutes. That's only during Friday evening traffic. Fine! You take her home then. Just don't hold her up too late. I know how you are when you want to sleep in. She'll be there till noon or later waiting on you."

"That's why I suggested the taxi if she doesn't want to wait," he snapped.

I was so done with this conversation. "Okay! By the way, thank you for the flowers and such a lovely evening. It meant a lot to me," I said as we pulled into the garage.

"Don't thank me; thank Brittany. It was her suggestion while we were riding to the house. She said I should make it like a real date with candy and flowers and stuff. So I tried it. The kids got a kick out of it." He chuckled.

I felt like I had just gotten a kick in my gut—from a donkey, no less. He did not have to tell me that he had no intentions of being romantic on his own.

"Well, then I'll be sure to thank Brittany."

I guess it was a good thing that I wasn't driving Brittany home that following morning. She was incoherent when I tried to wake her to let her know we were leaving and that Derrick would be driving her home later. I ended up leaving her a note on the refrigerator.

When I went to check on Derrick, he was snoring so hard that he didn't hear me say I was leaving. After I left, I kept getting this nagging feeling that I should have locked the door to his room to keep Brittany from wandering in and seeing Derrick sleeping with practically nothing on. She would be looking for someone in the house if she didn't go to the kitchen and see the note first.

Chapter 8

Derrick had been going around just a little too happy lately. He was scheduled to go to Atlanta, again, and it was supposedly for some university conference. If my brother was worth ten cents, I could have had him keep an eye out for me, but based on Derrick's level of happiness, I guessed JJ had something lined up that violated every code of marriage.

Since Derrick was going to go *again* and do his thing, I figured I could call Brittany to babysit. Maybe I could get dressed up and hit a happy hour networking event, or maybe even a movie just for me. If I had some real friends, I would have found a male-revue to go to and really let my hair down. But unfortunately, Brittany was going to be gone for the weekend, which meant I was stuck with the kids as always. I wasn't sure why I couldn't reach Kathy anymore. Brittany was supposed to be the backup, but lately, she was the only sitter.

"Would you be okay if I left Julie in charge for a few hours while I go out for a while? I really think we need to give her a chance to prove she can be responsible."

That was enough to wipe the happy smile clear off of Derrick's face. It also stopped him in his tracks long enough for me to realize he was about to pack his new silk boxers that I had yet to see him in.

"I already told you, Julie is too young. I want their mother home with them, giving them structure."

"And when exactly does the father get to hang around and give them structure?" I boldly asked.

"Look, Janelle, I am not going to get into it with you before I leave. This trip is very important, and I need to be in a good frame of mind."

"Funny you mention that. I noticed that you're in an exceptionally good mood for a so-called business trip. I take it you're meeting up with my brother to see what kind of mess the two of you can get into together, huh?" I tried to sound tough, but the truth of the matter was, I was fighting tears.

"JJ's in Europe somewhere working on new music. I won't even see him."

"So why the new boxers?"

"Oh, stop it! I am so sick of your insecurity. Now you're monitoring my underwear? Would you like to smell them when I return?"

"Would you like to smell mine when you return?" I shot back. I swear, I don't know where that came from.

Derrick charged at me and wrapped his hand around my throat, lifting me from my seat. He then released me just as quickly.

"I'm sorry. I'm sorry. I swore I'd never do that to you. Will you forgive me?" he asked, almost daring me to say, 'no.'

I absolutely did not—or would not—forgive him for that. How could I or why should I?

Instead of answering, I got up from my chaise lounge and ran into the bathroom. There was no way I'd tell him that choking me was okay. Common sense told me he was on his way to some fling with one of his bimbos, but choking me was a major violation of our marriage. There were many times I was afraid that he would strike me, but never did I think he'd actually go so far as to choke me—particularly when he was on his way to go violate the sanctity of our marriage.

"Janelle! Open this door! I need to know that you forgive me. Tell me you forgive me! Tell me now that you forgive me!" he yelled.

I couldn't believe his gall. He banged on the door as if he'd break it down any moment. Although there was a telephone in our master bathroom, I was uncertain if I should call the police or not. All I could think about was the damage the call would cause our family, so instead, I simply made the threat.

"Go away, Derrick, or I'm calling the police. Just finish packing and go on your stupid trip," I yelled through the door.

"Janelle, come out here right now. We need to talk. You need to tell me that you forgive me."

"I'm dialing. Leave me alone."

"Why are you being so stupid? I barely put my hand on you. If you weren't saying such stupid stuff, it would have never happened. I told you I want a peaceful home, so stop trying to make it a warzone with your stupidity."

So much for an apology.

"Hello, police?" I said loudly, pretending to be on the phone.

"Hello! Hello!" Derrick yelled out. He must have picked up the phone on the nightstand. I guess he was planning on providing his own warped account of events. "Why are you playing games, Janelle? You're not even on the phone."

I heard some chatter from the boys. I couldn't make out what was being said, but I did hear Derrick's words right before they screamed with excitement.

"Mommy's going to take you guys to a movie this weekend while I'm away. Anything you want to see. And here's twenty dollars each so you can have a big tub of popcorn and a big drink."

"Yeah!!" they screamed. "Daddy, you are the best!"

"We're not going to any movie until your dad returns from his quote-unquote business trip, and then he'll take you to see whatever you want. Mommy has things to do this weekend, and there won't be any time for a movie," I said, emerging from my hiding place with a red mark still around my neck from Derrick's grip.

The shocked look mixed with anger on his face was priceless. However, I didn't anticipate my boys turning on me. They clung to Derrick, begging him to "make" me take them.

"She'll take you," he assured them. "Stop crying. Go out and let me have a talk with Mommy."

I quickly made my way back into the bathroom and locked the door again. Then I turned on the water from each faucet to drown out any words he tried to speak through the door, along with the sounds of my own crying. I let the water continue to run until I could no longer hear him, which was a good fifteen minutes or so. I knew he had to get going, so I was hoping he would be gone when I opened the door. Instead, I felt the life being choked from me as quickly as I opened the door.

"You say what you will to me, but don't you upset my kids ever again. You're behaving stupid and immature all because of your insecurity. Who am I married to? That's all you should be concerning yourself with. They want what you already have, so stop acting stupid and taking it out on my children. You have plenty to keep you busy with the kids. You don't need to be running the streets like a common woman."

He finally let my neck go as I fell to the bathroom floor, while he went and sat on the bed to cry.

What did my stupid behind do? I got up and went to console him and apologized for my childish behavior.

Well, at least now I knew how to get my husband to show love and affection to me. He kissed me passionately and was even about to make love to me, but I was on yet another unscheduled period, which stopped him from going any further.

"You need to get that problem taken care of. A man has needs. I want to be with my wife sometimes. You're always bleeding. Get it fixed or something," he said, abruptly stopping any form of passion.

Chapter 9

felt like I was having an out-of-body experience. I couldn't imagine why I was in a gun range and shooting like a trained marksman. It was my fifth time in three weeks.

Derrick had been trying to get me to learn how to use a gun since we arrived in Memphis, due to the elevated crime level. I was always against the use of guns. I believed that if I had faith in God, that was all the protection I'd ever need for me and my family.

The funny thing was, I wasn't there because I was concerned with protection. There was just something driving me to learn to shoot and to do it right the first time, if it ever came to that. It may have been the whole choking incident that triggered that unquenchable thirst.

When Derrick returned from his trip, he came home long enough to pack a week's worth of clothes and he went to stay in a hotel for a week. His explanation was that I really needed time to think about losing him and the marriage. He told the kids that he would be away for business.

When he did return home, he pretty much stayed in a guest bedroom. He'd visit our bedroom long enough to see if I was bleeding, and if I wasn't, he'd want sex. No romance. Just hit it and return to the guest bedroom. He was supposedly still angry with me for taking him out of character and "causing him to choke me." Well, at least that was the reason he gave to me when I asked.

Still, he expected me to have his breakfast, coffee, dinner and his healthy snacks prepared. I was still expected to gather his dirty clothes to have them cleaned and hand back to him ready to wear. I was still expected to purchase all of his toiletries. No break from being his servant, yet he needed a break from me. Each day I found myself crying and then shifting into anger. I wondered if I was becoming bipolar. And then I found myself at the gun range, which somehow helped relieve my stress.

As I was taking my frustrations out on my imaginary target, I heard an oddly familiar voice say, "Practicing to take the hubby out, I see."

I wasn't sure if I was hearing right, but then I turned to see ol' Willard standing with his arms folded above his gut, making it evident that he hadn't been hitting that gym lately—or ever. He wore a wicked smile that let me know that he was hoping to have something to report back to Derrick. In that moment, I was half tempted to hire a PI just to find out who his wife was, so I could let her know of his shenanigans and get him out of my business, but then I figured there might be some code amongst PI's, and it would get back to him while I'd be the butt of the joke.

When I removed my ear covers, he repeated, "Practicing to take the hubby out, huh?"

"What?" was all I could think to say.

"I can see the rage and the precision. We like to call that 'Hubby Practice.'"

"Go away, you old fool! Don't you have one of your wife's family members to keep you occupied? Shoo, you pesky old fly!"

"I could give you a few pointers if you'd like."

"So, what you're saying is, you want me to be better at shooting my husband?"

"Oh, so you are practicing for the hubby?"

"I never said that. Don't try to twist my words. Once again, that was your presumption. Then you offer to help me perfect what you presume."

"You never said that you were trying to dig up dirt on your husband, but we both know that was the purpose of your visit. And now, here you are, practicing for the execution of the husband who is doing you dirty." He laughed.

I stood for a hot second to think on his admission that my husband was doing me wrong.

I smiled. "Thanks for the free information. I'll be sure to let my husband know that you told me while I was at the gun range, practicing how to use the gun he purchased for our home. Now don't you feel stupid?"

He looked confused. He couldn't figure out what he had said wrong, so I graciously told him, "You just said my husband is doing me dirty, which is why you believe I'm practicing at the range. No, dear, I didn't think my husband was doing anything wrong. But now that you mentioned it, I'll just have to ask him about it."

"I never said he was doing you—You know what? Think what you want," he said as his eyes shifted to a young girl who had just entered the range looking lost and confused.

My eyes followed his. "Another of your wife's family members?"

"For your information, I provide training to people to help them improve their skills, which is why I offered you assistance. It's part of my business."

"If you say so."

As the girl got closer to us, Willard quickly said, "I have to go."

"Don't you want to introduce your lady friend?"

The girl came to Willard with a big smile and reached up to kiss him. He tried to pull his face back before she could make contact with his lips.

"Hey, baby!" she innocently said, and then cut her eyes toward me. "Oh, I thought this was going to be a private lesson. You know I get nervous with other people around."

I intruded their private moment to cause Willard further discomfort. "Hello, I'm Janelle, and you are?"

Willard looked like he saw a ghost. "We really have to be going now."

"What? I just got here. Why we gotta leave?" the young lady protested before she turned to me. "Hello, I'm Sasha. Nice to meet you."

I smiled. "You wouldn't be related to Stacy, would you? You look so much alike," I lied. I just threw her name out, fishing.

"Oh, you know my cousin? She used to work for Willard."

"Yeah, we met at his office a while back. I'll let you two get on to your business now. I'm sure you came to practice and not chat," I said, smiling big at Willard.

Another family member. *Oh, I can't wait to meet his wife.*

"Yes, let's get to work," he agreed, trying to lead Sasha away.

"Nice meeting you, Janelle," she yelled as he ushered her away.

After that, she made another attempt to get a kiss from Willard, that time wrapping her arms around his neck. As far away as they were, I could still see the beads of sweat on his forehead.

As I resumed my target practice, I had to think of yet another story I'd tell Derrick when the blabbermouth decided he would tell on me yet again. If I thought I could get away with it, I'd pump ol' Mr. Willard Barker full of lead, especially for taking up the little time I had to myself before I had to get the kids for their activities. I actually rearranged client business to indulge in this moment, and it was wrecked by Willard.

I also couldn't forget about Willard's unintended admission of my husband doing me dirty. If I had half a nerve, I would have told Derrick I was at the gun range because his friend told me he'd been doing me wrong. That would've straightened his wrong out, real fast. The thought made me smile.

Chapter 10

was so happy when my mom told me she was coming to visit me for a couple of days. It was a very rare treat, but I figured it must have been something serious to make her take a trip. I'm not sure why it didn't occur to me, HOW she was supposed to get from Brentwood to Collierville. Needless to say, my heart sank when she showed up to my door accompanied by Janae. Derrick was also looking forward to the visit from my mom, but when I let him know that Janae showed up as well, suddenly he had a business trip to take. It was *unexpected*.

Janae gave me her usual, "You're stupid!" look the minute I fixed my mouth to say Derrick wouldn't be joining us for dinner because he had to take an unexpected trip to Louisville, Kentucky for some recruiting program.

"Oh, how disappointing," my mom said.

"So let me see if I understand this correctly: a school dean takes unexpected recruiting trips that he doesn't get a whole day's notice for, huh?" Janae said before releasing her exaggerated laugh.

"Mom! Why would you bring this cancer with you? You know she works my last nerve," I childishly pouted, just like when we were kids.

"Janelle, don't you say things like that about your sister. You'd be sorry if anything were to happen to her," Momma scolded.

I turned my head to roll my eyes when I saw the cheesy grin on Janae's face. I didn't want to be disrespectful to my mother, but sometimes she got on my nerves too, especially when she was treating Janae like a saint. Yes, she was correct when she said that I'd be sorry if anything were to happen to my only sister, but still.

If Derrick's ducking out on dinner with my mom wasn't bad enough, Brittany turned around and called to tell me she wasn't feeling well because of bad cramps. I swore to myself that I was going to find another babysitter, since Brittany was becoming so unreliable. Then again, I had to cut her some slack since she had really just made it to adulthood. In essence, she still behaved like a teenager, although her body was anything but.

The following day, Mom, Janae, and I decided to do a little shopping and lunch. Typically, my mom was a pro at hiding her feelings, but it was obvious that something had been weighing on her since she had arrived.

"Mom, what's going on with you? I've noticed something wrong since you got here," I asked.

"After forty-five years of marriage, she's probably now convinced that it's not all that it's cracked up to be. You ready for a divorce, Mom?" Janae insensitively asked.

"Bite your tongue, Janae! Don't you talk foolishness about your father," Momma snapped, fighting tears.

"I didn't say anything bad about Daddy. I'm just talking about this whole marriage nonsense that you all pressure Janelle to stay in, even when it should be taken out to pasture and shot."

"Always the cynic. Mind your business!"

"Hush that noise, girl!" Momma snapped at me.

By this moment, I was about ready for both of them to head back east. They were both riding my last nerve. The combination of Janae and Momma had me contemplating ordering something stronger than the Shirley Temple I had been slowly sipping on, as if it contained alcohol.

"Your daddy has prostate cancer. He didn't want anyone to know about it, but I'm tired of carrying this secret burden all by myself," Momma blurted out.

Janae and I both sat there stunned with open mouths, waiting for flies.

"Momma," was all I could say when I was finally able to speak.

"How? When? Where?" Janae asked.

Momma's face was stoic. It was at that very moment that I realized why I kept noticing a rapid aging in her face. She seemed worn down. I won't lie. I, too, wondered if her marriage was as horrible as mine, and if it was, how she survived forty-five years of it.

I remember a time when my dad thought he was a ladies' man, and he'd tell JJ that he could never turn in his man card, not even for marriage. At the same time, he would always speak of adultery being the greatest sin in the Bible. But then again, my daddy would twist up the Bible like it was nobody's business. He also used to ask us how we'd feel if he took on other wives like the men of the Bible. Yep! Momma had to suffer through all of his nonsense, and now this.

"Daddy's been sick about eight or nine months now. He didn't tell me about it until four months ago. He made me promise not to tell anyone, but now with it spreading, I don't feel we should be keeping this from our children any longer. We don't have to tell anyone else, but you have a right to know."

"Have you spoken with JJ yet?" Janae asked.

"No, I haven't told your brother. I'm not sure how he's going to take it. I figured at least you girls would have each other to get through this ordeal. I don't think he'll take the news as well," she answered with sadness.

"Momma, you can't *not* tell him. That will make matters worse," I calmly admonished.

"I know. I just don't know when or how. There's no telling how your daddy's gonna feel when I let him know that I told you two. He's going to feel I betrayed him."

"Momma, please stop worrying about Daddy being upset with you. You did right to tell his children," Janae said. She was obviously angry, but was trying not to upset Momma any further. "It would have been insane for you to wait for him to be buried before telling your children. Momma, you shouldn't have to do this alone. And as for JJ, I'll fly down to Atlanta when he gets back and I'll sit him down."

Momma smiled. "You'd do that for me?"

"I'd lay down my life for you, woman," Janae said, getting up to give Momma a big hug.

"That's why you're my perfect angel," Momma said, reawakening my age-old inferiority complex to my younger sister. I had never been titled 'perfect' or 'angel,' but this wasn't the time to discuss the topic.

"I know Derrick's going to be devastated when you tell him," Momma said, catching me off guard.

"Oh, I hadn't planned on telling him," I answered.

"Why would you keep something like this from your husband? Doesn't he have the right to know?" Janae disingenuously asked.

I know she was just trying to get me to admit that we were having problems. Otherwise, she'd be the first one on the line to encourage withholding information from my husband. Now she was acting like she was concerned about his feelings. Ha!

"I just feel he has so much going on right now with this new job. This position has him traveling and working almost around the clock. I'm sure telling him about Daddy would just add to his pressures. I would hate for him to mess up his important position," I lied—or half lied.

"Momma, have you ever heard of a Dean of Business traveling like that? Particularly in this age of technology? Janelle doesn't feel Derrick needs to know about Daddy because she thinks he's cheating on her."

I was stunned. Janae could be so callous at times.

"Janelle! Now that's just foolish. You're gonna sit your husband down and tell him about Daddy," Momma scolded me. "You don't punish him because you think he's being unfaithful to you. You don't have any proof, and even if you did, it's your own fault for allowing another woman to waltz in and walk away with your husband. Your husband has been telling you forever to get yourself fixed, with all that bleeding mess. How long do you expect him to wait on you being so hard-headed? That's just selfish and inconsiderate. I had to do what I had to do to keep my husband happy, and what didn't happen was another woman getting to walk in and take my husband and the father of my children."

"But at least you respect your vows of staying in sickness and health. You think it's right for my husband to punish me for being sick? I didn't do this to myself. Do you think I like hemorrhaging like I do, almost to the point where I feel like I'll pass out any moment? I hate this affliction just as much as he does, but that's no reason to treat me like dirt," I snapped as a multitude of tears fell. I didn't mean to actually admit any wrongdoing in my marriage, but then again, it seemed as if I was the only one in denial about it. "You wouldn't leave Daddy now that he's sick, would you?"

"Your daddy is taking the steps necessary to fix his sickness, but you—you're not trying to help yourself. That is selfish and inconsiderate. You can't have my sympathy. You think I don't know your husband's unfaithful to you? I know he is, and I don't blame him, and neither can you. It's your fault. Go get yourself fixed!" Momma yelled. I was sure every surrounding table now knew my husband was unfaithful. "The man has needs and desires, and it's your job to see that they are satisfied in every way."

"Momma, you're not seriously sitting here suggesting that Janelle should be okay with a cheating husband, are you?" Janae asked in my defense.

"I didn't say she should be okay with it. I said she should do what she must to keep him satisfied."

"And how exactly do you suggest I get fixed when all responsibilities fall solely upon my shoulders? I have a business, children, family, and a husband that sucks up every bit of my minutes. I'm only one person without a drop of help. When am I supposed to go get myself fixed?" At this point, I was the one raising my voice. The unfazed look in my mother's face caused me to abruptly get up and make a mad dash for the ladies' room. I didn't want to be in my mother's presence any more that day. I needed for her to go home and leave my confused life be.

When I came out of the ladies' room, I ran into a young man, maybe ten years my junior.

"For what it's worth, any man who treats you wrong would need his head examined," he said. When he noticed my embarrassment, he said, "I'm sorry. I didn't mean to embarrass you, but I just wanted you to know you have at least one ally in this place. I take it that was your mom, and trust me, I have firsthand knowledge on overbearing, embarrassing mothers. My mom probably has yours beat, hands down."

I couldn't help but laugh. The thought of anyone's mother being more embarrassing than mine was frightening. I also appreciated having an ally for a change.

"Kenny. Kenny Waldron," he said, extending a hand.

"Janelle. Janelle Roberts," I replied, accepting his hand.

Is this cheating? I felt an electrical sensation shoot up my arm and down my spine. Kenny was suddenly handsome. Gorgeous. I don't think I had viewed a man as handsome, other than Derrick, since we first met. It just seemed so forbidden, as did the moment.

"Nice to make your acquaintance, Janelle Roberts. I hate to seem rude, but I was in the middle of a business lunch with a potential client. It just bothered me to see what you were going through out there, and I wanted to check up on you since I understand all too well."

Wow! I was so flattered. Amazed.

"Why thank you, Mr. Waldron. That was very thoughtful of you."

"Please, Kenny—I insist."

"Kenny." I smiled. "And what is your business, if you don't mind my asking? I am also a business owner."

"Oh wow! This is great! I do financial and business development. I've been working for myself since I finished my MBA ten years ago. I do pretty well for my clients and have grown multi-billion-dollar portfolios."

"That is very impressive." I dug into my purse for one of my cards. He laughed when he saw the same title on my business card. I was too embarrassed to admit that I didn't have anywhere close to his success rate. Thankfully, he didn't ask.

"This is great. Maybe one day we could break bread together and talk shop. I would love to refer my overflow of clients to you if you aren't too booked up," he said, handing me his card.

"Looking forward to it." Unfortunately, I couldn't offer him any of my overflow clients. With my schedule, I barely had any more clients.

"Again, it was great to make you acquaintance, but I really must get back out there. This is one of those multi-billion-dollar deals. I don't want to blow this one."

"Yes! Sure, I understand. Good luck, and thank you again." I stood there smiling, as I held his card near my nose and shamelessly inhaled the scent that lingered from its owner.

It was as if Kenny was a breastplate on me after I rejoined my mother and sister, who seemed happy in my absence. They were enjoying themselves, not at all concerned with the misery that caused me to run to the bathroom.

"Feel better?" my mom asked as she did when I was a kid and she'd sit idly as I cried out whatever was bothering me.

At that same moment, I made eye contact with Kenny from across the restaurant with his clients. He winked at me as he continued talking to his clients, who were looking at the papers in front of them. I smiled and answered my mother, "Much better."

"Good. I'm ready to get out of here. I'm tired. I need a nap now that I have a break from your father."

I laughed. I definitely understood the need. I wondered how old I'd be when I'd finally get to steal a nap.

I don't know if the sun was shining before I ran into the bathroom, but suddenly, the day appeared beautiful. It didn't even bother me when Derrick called to say he'd be stuck in Louisville an extra night. I didn't even worry myself over the fact that he somehow didn't need to come back home to pack for this unexpected trip.

Chapter 11

So, I'm in the grocery store, thumping for fresh produce, checking dates on dairy, and shuffling groceries on the shelves for the freshest items, just minding my own business, and who bothers me at the seafood counter? Carmen's pew-mate, Jocelyn.

Carmen always seemed to have her little loyal entourage in church each Sunday morning and Wednesday night at Bible study. They hardly attended church for the word of God, but to see what relationship they could infiltrate.

These women were so low-down that I heard a couple of them had been intimately involved with the Senior Pastor Hill *and* the Junior Pastor Hill. I believe Jocelyn was one of the ones to receive 'special prayer,' directly from the Senior Pastor Hill. I heard he treated his women well and showered them with expensive gifts. Surely, they were being treated from our tithes and offerings.

But in all fairness to Jocelyn, rumors were endless in our church. And poor Brittany was the most talked about person in the congregation. According to the rumors, there wasn't a man in there who hadn't been with her. The young boys said she was the one to go to when you wanted to give up your virginity. It didn't help her cause that she was always pointing out how big her butt was getting. It really wasn't, but she drew negative attention by making everyone look at her body.

Ironically, it seemed that Carmen's entire clique was in possession of bodies that would cause other women to be insecure, myself included. Supposedly,

Carmen had a granddaughter, which meant she no spring chicken, but she didn't look a day over thirty. Jocelyn had a seventeen-year-old son, but she looked like she was in her twenties. I knew one thing, as youthful and physically attractive as they were, they all behaved like juvenile delinquents.

As long as I had lived in Memphis, this was my first time running into any of them outside of church. Based on their behaviors, I would have pegged the lot of them to be residents of some ghetto, and certainly not close enough to be shopping in my favorite gourmet grocery store, less than two miles from my home.

"Sister Janelle, how are you?" the fake asked me when I turned to the calling of my name.

I gave her one my fake smiles but almost jumped out of my skin when she came and hugged me as if we were besties.

"Did you guys just move near here? I haven't seen you here before. Derrick didn't tell me we might be neighbors," she said.

Hmm, not "Brother Derrick" or "Brother Roberts," huh?

"No, we've been here since moving to Memphis."

"Wow, this is wonderful. I'll definitely have to have you over one evening for cocktails or something."

"Can't imagine ever being so desperate for friends or company," was what I wanted to say. Instead, I said, "Sounds delightful, but honestly, with my busy schedule, I wouldn't see the time."

"Girl, you better make time." She laughed as if we were really friends. "No sense in the guys always out having fun, doing what makes them happy. You may as well live just the same."

Now, was that her throwing shade about my husband?

"Oh, I didn't know you were married as well," I said, taking note of the plural on guys.

"Shoot no! Been there, done that! My ex didn't know how to keep his pants zipped while I sat at home raising our son. Nope, I've been enjoying the single life for the past eight years. Much better benefits as well."

"Oh really?" I asked, intrigued to hear more of her dirt.

"Girl, yeah! I have yet to pay a mortgage payment on my six-thousand-square-foot home, or a car note on my Benz truck. My son has been in private school for the past five years and has done so well there that he's getting a full-ride scholarship for college. I get to do—and I mean this literally—whatever or whomever I feel like, whenever I feel like."

"Wow! Neat!" I smiled, still in phony mode.

"We all make good money with our businesses, and we bank our coins."

"Oh, really? What kind of business do you have?" I asked. Honestly, I took her for a hooker, since she had men paying for everything.

"I own three childcare centers throughout Memphis. I'm actually working on franchising now."

"Wow!" Now that was a genuine "wow." I was blown away.

"You already know that Carmen owns the Catfish Shack, but she also owns a dessert café and a rib shack. Each of her spots has her earning hand-over-fist. Frieda owns three hair salons and two barber shops, and Maggie has a couple of upscale clothing boutiques. I'm not sure if you've met Jada, since she hardly makes time for church anymore, but she buys and flips houses throughout the entire state. Man, she's getting paid, big time!"

"That's amazing," was all I could bring myself to say. I truly was blown away. I would've even been proud of them and their success, but it was kind of hard to get past their ugly and disrespectful ways when it came to my marriage.

Truth is, I was feeling a bit professionally inadequate compared to these women. Being married with three children caused the sacrifice of my professional self. If Derrick had said he was leaving me tomorrow, I wasn't sure how I'd manage on my own with the kids. I wouldn't even know how to get more clients.

"So, say you'll stop by sometime for drinks," she persisted.

"Honestly, I couldn't. But I appreciate the thought."

"Girl, you better stop letting your man have all the fun while you sit up at home like Mother Hen. Derrick comes by sometimes with some of the other fellas just to have a few brews, watch some sports, or shoot some pool. And he certainly didn't miss my annual pool party, like you did."

I was sure that the vein in the center of my forehead was protruding and visibly thumping, as Jocelyn stood studying my entire demeanor while she spoke. It was clear that she wanted to see me flinch as she ratted on my husband. I refused to give her the satisfaction. Instead I smiled.

"Speaking of Carmen, have you been by her Catfish Shack yet? 'Cause you should make it a point of hanging out there sometime. You'd be surprised by the things you'll see there."

I didn't know whether to let that fly over my head or reach up and catch it.

"I know Derrick hangs out there a bit. I don't spy on my husband. It's not necessary, but I appreciate your concern," I said insincerely.

"So you're okay with Derrick and Carmen being together?" she just came straight out and asked. No more gloves or subtlety.

"Excuse me? Together? Together like what?" I snapped, unable to mask my growing anger while she continued to play the sincere friend concerned with my well-being.

"Janelle, that's why I told you to go hang out there. Now, she assured me that she's not trying to be with him, but brother be trying to push up hard on my girl. I'm just saying. Perhaps if he was to run into you there, he might back off a bit. I mean, you see how he is even when we're in church." Jocelyn paused to pull out her phone. "Check this out. These are from my house one night."

I really didn't want to look, but I couldn't help myself. There were so many pictures on her phone, but there were definitely plenty of my husband having a good time and a few of him inappropriately holding onto different young girls, looking happier than a kid on Christmas morning. I'm not sure why the others didn't bother me half as much as the ones with him all over Carmen at her restaurant, all playful. One picture showed him trying to reach his hand either between her thighs or underneath her short dress, while she seemed to actually be pulling away from him while laughing. In all of the pictures, he was oblivious that his photo was being taken.

"I know this must seem like I'm being mean and hateful by showing you these, but I'm actually trying to help you. There is no reason you should be living like some hermit. You better get your life."

"You're right. I *am* thinking you're just trying to be mean and hateful right now," I said, fighting tears.

"Okay, if I'm being mean, then what does that make your husband, who is obviously not thinking about you when he's away from you? And what does that make you—the one trying to turn a blind eye from the facts?"

"I don't care what those pictures show. My husband would never cheat on me. Him being playful is not cheating. Nice try."

I took my cart and started rushing away, but when I heard her shout out, "Even I've been with him, fool. You know, with that of blood issue you got, and all."

At first I stopped, ready to turn back to confront her, but since it was getting harder for me to breathe, I just left the store without my groceries. I managed to hold my tears until I pulled out of the parking lot.

I immediately called Derrick to demand an explanation. He seemed to neatly explain everything off as being innocent, even the photo of him grabbing for Carmen's goodies. He said she took his car key from the table and put them between her legs, telling him if he wanted to go home, then he had better get his key the best way he could. I believed him, as it seemed quite convenient for Jocelyn to be snapping pictures right at that moment. He said he innocently mentioned the issue of bleeding one Sunday in church, when he said that we were believing for a healing just the same as the woman in the Bible.

However, when I asked if he had been intimate with Jocelyn as she stated, he said, "Janelle, get off of my phone with your foolish insecurities," and then hung up on me. Worse, he decided to stay out that night and came home at the time I wake up to get everyone together. He said he stayed out to teach me a lesson about letting other people get into my head and into our marriage. As much as I hated his punishments, I had to admit, he was absolutely correct. I had no business entertaining Jocelyn or any of her friends' shenanigans.

They had no respect for the church. Surely, nothing she said came with good intention. And I refused to allow my insecurities to question why Derrick was jumping into the shower before I could make it in. Nope! No questions, no more.

Chapter 12

Upon the advice of everyone, I went to my gynecologist to finally do something about the constant hemorrhaging. Well, in reality, it took my iron level to drop so dangerously low that I passed out at home. Thankfully, I was alone when it happened. I could just hear everyone calling me stupid, had they known. I honestly didn't believe I would have received one single word of sympathy. They'd say I brought it upon myself.

The doctor said I need to have surgery as soon as possible, but surgery was not an option with my schedule. Plus, that surgery seemed so final. Choice B was also a surgical option, but more like a temporary fix. Instead, I foolishly opted for choice C, which was hormone pills to help stop the bleeding, and possibly shrink some of the fibroids facilitating the bleeding. Lo and behold, I managed to make it a whole two weeks without bleeding. While that might seem like a good thing, it wasn't.

Prior to the pills, I barely had any sex drive. Just the mention of sex made me think of all of my other tasks and chores. But since starting the medication, I could hardly think about anything else. Even worse, it wasn't my husband I was thinking about. It was the young guy I met a while back and had yet to hear from or call. Kenny. All kinds of filthy thoughts about him commandeered my "pure" mind. In all my years with Derrick, never did I think it was even possible for me to think about another man. Especially intimately.

It was a Thursday night and Derrick decided to go to bed at ten o'clock. I just knew what that meant, and I was actually happy for a change about the opportunity to be with my husband. He hadn't touched or attempted to touch me in the whole two weeks I was flow-free. Instead, I was faced with one rejection behind another. I wasn't sure how much more rejection my poor ego would stand. But surely, Derrick in bed by ten meant an evening of intimacy. I couldn't get the household settled fast enough.

I sifted through my drawer for something sexy to put on after my shower. I was going to make sure my husband remembered why he chose me to marry. Oddly, Derrick didn't mumble a peep the entire time I was in the room. Not even when I turned on a low light so he could see me before I climbed into the bed. When I crawled into our king-sized bed and moved up behind him, I noticed he was wrapped up in flannel pajamas and a heavy velour robe, bundled up snugly underneath layers of covers and blankets.

For a hot minute, I pondered the thought of him being sick, which was the only other time he went to bed early. But since he hadn't mentioned anything or made any of his usual demands, I dismissed the notion. Still, I couldn't understand why the layers and him being in bed so early.

I kissed him gently on the back of his neck and under his ear, as I attempted to get a hand inside of his pajama top. He had an undershirt on under it, to my dismay. Infiltrating Fort Knox seemed easier, but I was horny and determined.

"Janelle! Would you stop it!!" he yelled in a fit of rage. "I don't feel well. Why must you be so inconsiderate? You need to go and tell that doctor to help you fix whatever has caused you to become so inconsiderate lately. You know I only go to bed early when I don't feel well. My goodness! You are becoming ridiculous."

"I'm ridiculous for trying to be with my husband, who has put me off for over two weeks now? Did you tell me you were sick? NO! No, you did not!" And without fail, the tears poured from my eyes. Words could not describe how foolish I was feeling in that moment. "I want a divorce!" I yelled out of nowhere.

Oh my! Wherever did that come from? I didn't mean it—at least I don't think I did.

Derrick laughed. He was amused by my humiliation. "Girl, go to sleep."

"I'm not sleepy and you can't tell me to go to sleep as if I'm some small child. I'll stay up all night if I feel like it. You are not the boss of me. I write the rules for my own life. Yeah, from now on, I go by my own set of rules, and I'm my own boss, and I say I don't feel like going to sleep," I said, sounding every bit like a five-year-old.

"Okay, then go bring me some tea. My throat is scratchy and I'm cold. Bring me the thermometer while you're up."

"I want a divorce, Derrick!" I repeated, still unsure if I meant it.

"No, you're not getting a divorce and giving your sister the satisfaction of saying your marriage failed. Now, go get me some tea and a thermometer. I think I have a temperature."

"Everyone has a temperature, fool!" I said, still pouting. I don't EVER remember calling Derrick a fool or any other name for that matter. I didn't know what was happening to me.

He laughed again. "Fool, huh? Yeah, I'm just gonna chalk that slip-up to those pills you've been taking. Now, get up and get that tea and thermometer like I told you to, and keep in mind, this will be the last time I ask you."

I got bold. I stood from the bed like Wonder Woman and put both hands on my waist, daring him to come with his best shot. For the moment, I was serious about that divorce, and I didn't even care what Janae would think or say—for the moment.

Derrick lifted up on an elbow and looked me over as if he actually appreciated what he was seeing. "Wow! You look beautiful. All of that was for me? Man, I'm so sorry about being sick right now," he said, seducing me with his eyes.

And that was all it took. I smiled. I was glad he noticed my efforts.

He continued. "Baby, if I was feeling well, you'd see an animal tonight. Definitely when I get better. Now this is the wife that I miss. Do you forgive me for being so onerous tonight? You know I'm not the nicest when I'm feeling under the weather. I was trying not to bother you earlier while you were baking those cupcakes for Bryce's bake sale tomorrow. So I just came and got into the bed. I'm sorry."

He patted the bed in front of where he was lying. "Come sit."

I obliged.

"You forgive me?" he asked before gently kissing my lips. "Oh, I shouldn't be kissing you. I don't want to make you sick too."

"Thank you for taking notice. I want our marriage to get better, and now that the hemorrhaging stopped, I thought that maybe . . . you know..."

"Thank you for not giving up on us. You are definitely my rock. I wish there was no such thing as sickness," he said, seeming genuinely distressed about not being able to fully appreciate my lingerie. "Now, if it's not too much, could you get me that thermometer and a cup of tea?"

This time I gave him all he needed, with a smile. I even got him some Tylenol when the thermometer showed a high temperature. I felt soooo stupid for acting soooo childish.

For the four days to follow, I nursed my husband back to health, despite all of my other duties. And without fail, I ended up sick as a result, with no one to take care of me. I actually had to send for Brittany to help with some of the stuff I couldn't do around the house. She graciously stayed over for a couple of days while I recuperated. Needless to say, Derrick would not chance getting sick again, and he stayed in the guest room in the basement while I recovered.

I was looking forward to my recovery, because all I could think about was the love I'd be making with my husband when I was better. Instead, he wanted to wait an extra week just to make sure all of the sickness was gone. But then Mother Nature cruelly appeared, making me the butt of her joke. The pills stopped working and the doctor wanted to try some others, since I still wasn't open to surgery yet. That was definitely a trial and error period in my life.

Chapter 13

hank you so much for coming and helping me with the boys, Brittany. You were such a big help when I was sick. I'm not sure why it never occurred to me to have you help out with other times, since Derrick and I hardly make it to date night anymore."

"Glad to help out, Janelle."

Janelle? What happened to "Miss Janelle" or "Mrs. Roberts?" Just Janelle, as if we're equals now. Okay paranoid mind, STOP IT!! These hormone pills will be the death of me. I can't even think straight anymore.

I found myself staring at Brittany's healthy-sized bottom. I'd heard her say a million times, how it was getting bigger and bigger, and I'd always tell her that it was just her imagination. However, as I sat at the kitchen island, working on my laptop while she prepared dinner, I definitely observed an increase in her assets—top and bottom.

"What?" she innocently asked when she caught me taking inventory.

I shook my head. "It's nothing."

"I guess you noticed too, yes?" she asked, patting her behind.

"I must admit, I do see an increase for sure. You say it so much, but this time it actually looks like it. Even up top. Are you pregnant?" I just boldly asked. I won't lie, her newly growing assets suddenly seemed threatening to me and my marriage. Before, I just looked at her as a kid, but now she looked every bit a threatening woman.

She looked panicked. "Oh God, I hope not. Derrick would kill me."

Derrick? That sounded like fight words.

"Excuse me?!" I yelled, as I stood up.

"Oh, no—I meant to say with school. I told him I'd attend school next fall, and he's been helping me to find some scholarships. A pregnancy would be such a setback," she said, sure to keep the island between us as she spoke.

"Oh, okay," I said, calming down. *Yeah, these hormone pills got me tripping, big time.*

"You really think I might be pregnant? I was wondering why my breasts were getting bigger too."

"Have you missed a period?"

"No, not really. I don't be looking for one. I figure it comes when it come."

I had a blank stare on my face. I could never understand why people too stupid to keep up with their cycles would think they'd be smart enough to have sex, let alone raise a child. But, I to cut her some slack since her mother was killed and I was certain Mother Hill was incapable of having an intelligent conversation about the birds and the bees.

"Have you ever been to a gynecologist before?" I asked, praying she was at least familiar with the terminology.

"I haven't been to one yet, but I've heard of them."

"That's where you get birth control if you're going to be sexually active."

She laughed as if I had just told a joke. "Oh, my other doctor gave me pills for that. I didn't like the way they made me feel, so I stopped taking them."

I was certainly able to relate. I hated taking those hormone pills.

"But you have to take something, Brittany."

"I've heard if you make a guy take it out, you won't get pregnant."

I couldn't help myself. I burst out laughing. "That's what young dumb boys will tell you, and then they'll be nowhere to be found when you're pregnant."

That time it was Brittany who looked like she'd come over the counter to hurt me. "It's not just young boys. I'm not as dumb as you think I am. I be with older men who tell me that."

"Aww, sweetheart, I'm sorry. I didn't mean to belittle you. These are things Derrick and I have to talk about with Julie, for whenever that time may come. However, as for those older men, they should know better. You're just barely a child yourself."

"But I'm not a child anymore. When I was a child, it didn't stop my stepfather, which is why I'm glad my dad killed my mother, because she let my stepfather do whatever he wanted. Oh, did I forget to mention his friends too?"

I was too stunned for words. That was the first time I had heard the whole story. I would never dare ask. While a hardened Brittany didn't seem to shed a tear, I was broken to tears.

"I am so sorry, Brittany."

"You don't have to be. It's not like you did it. Why you think all them men say all those things about me in the church? 'Cause some of them were my stepfather's friends."

"Are you serious?! Do your grandparents know that you sit in church with some of the same men who molested you? I think you should make them aware."

"Nothing's a secret. They know. Grandpa Hill said every saint in the church has a sinful past, but it's not my place to interfere with redemption. They said I need to be forgiving so the enemy can't have a hold on my soul." She shrugged her shoulders. "I forgave them and we moved on with our lives. And to show there was no hard feelings, I've even slept with two of them since. Now I feel like I hold the power. They be begging, but I told them to leave me alone before I tell their wives."

"Brittany!" was all I could say.

"Stop crying. There's no need to be upset. No one is making me do anything I don't want to do, ever again."

"What are you going to do if you're pregnant? Could it be one of theirs"

"If I'm pregnant, I'm keeping my baby and its daddy will just have to accept it. But to answer your other question, no, neither of them are the daddy. They were from last year."

I sat doing some quick mental math.

"Uh, but you're just eighteen now. Last year you were seventeen."

"Yeah, and?" she callously asked. "Grandpa said forgive them and let it go, so now that I hold the power, I ain't got a problem with it, and neither should anyone else."

I so desperately wanted to ask if she even knew who the father could be. I was starting to believe all the many rumors I'd heard about Brittany. I looked at her as some poor, misunderstood victim of her stepfather's abuse. Not that it makes it any better, but I was glad it was a stepfather and not her biological father, as we previously believed.

"Who has to forgive what?" Bryce came into the kitchen asking. "I'm hungry. When's dinner?"

"Mind your business. Dinner should be ready in a few. Doesn't it smell super delicious?" I asked.

"Yeah! Did Miss Brittany cook again? I like her food. I wish she could cook for us every day," he said, and she smiled while I was struck with jealousy. "Can you move here for good and cook every day."

"Aw, how sweet. I'm sure your mom is a great cook too," Brittany defended me.

"Not as good as you. Sorry, Mommy, but even Daddy said Miss Brittany is a super-duper cooker."

"Cook," I corrected, not the least bit amused by his collection of words.

Another mental note: FIRE BRITTANY ASAP!

I was even more annoyed when my dear husband came sauntering in early enough for a hot dinner prepared by Brittany. I couldn't remember the last time he was home in time for a hot dinner with me and the children on a weekday.

While we were eating, I received an unusual call from my mother, whose rule I've implemented into my own household: No phone calls during dinner. I figured it had to be important. I learned my dad was in the hospital.

Now, while I did appreciate Derrick's firm offer to drive us to Nashville, I had to remind him that the kids were due for exams in school, along with their other activities, and we couldn't say how long we would need to be gone. Besides, I wanted him to get a dose of a day or two of my everyday life.

Brittany, bless her wayward heart, offered to hang around and help out while I was gone. I told her that there was already too much church gossip going around, and we wouldn't want to give anyone anything to talk about. Derrick actually agreed with me. Who knew? He said he'd call her a taxi to get her home after she finished cleaning the kitchen. I was satisfied with that.

Chapter 14

I never thought the day would come when I would say it, but I *really* wanted to just pick up a stick and beat my mom.

I ran off during dinner, leaving my husband vulnerable to some loose woman-child in my home, to take a three-hour drive alone. I got all the way to the hospital to find out that visiting hours were over and had to wait around worried until the next afternoon, only to find out that my dad had hemorrhoids.

Wait! Get this—he doesn't even have prostate cancer or any other cancer for that matter. Come to find out, he and Momma were getting busy right before he went in for his exam all those months ago, and his PSA levels were super high. Daddy refused to go in for any further testing. The so-called spreading of his cancer was the doctor telling him his gastric upset was an ulcer.

So what did my momma do? She got on Google to do research and tried to play doctor. Did I fail to mention that Momma is sixty-eight years old? She told him that an ulcer meant the cancer was spreading to his bowels. In one sense, I was thankful for Daddy's hemorrhoids, because that's what caused the hospital to keep him and further investigate the fictitious prostate cancer. I was so disgusted to learn of my parents' DAILY sex life. I was lucky to get it in monthly, let alone daily. So despite his doctor telling him to refrain from any activities at least two days prior to testing, he decided to have sex right before the exam, "Just in case."

AAAHG!

I could have left to return home after learning about the hemorrhoids, but I decided to hang around in Nashville an extra night just to make Derrick have to do some work for a change. I was tempted to stay a third night, but when I heard Janae was on her way, I decided to get out of Dodge. There was no way I was going to subject myself to having her and Momma teaming up on me again. Although the hospital continued to keep Daddy just to one-hundred percent clear him, I planned on being gone before he got home and before Janae showed up.

I took my sweet time driving back to Memphis. I treated myself to a delightful lunch without any interruptions or the need to rush. Four and a half hours into my three-hour drive home, Derrick called to tell me I needed to hurry up to get home because he had a late meeting and would be unable to get the kids. Momma was gracious enough to call my darling husband when I left Brentwood, to let him know to be on the lookout for me. He had the audacity to accuse me of being untrustworthy before he hung up on me—right before I heard a woman start talking. I couldn't make out the voice or what was said, but the way he ended the call prompted me to call him back. Each of the three attempts I dialed, the call was sent to voicemail.

If I had time, I would have done a drive-by to his job. I hadn't been allowed to visit him at work since . . . since . . . Wow! I had never been to his office in Memphis. The closest thing to being invited to his office was when he wanted me to enter that stupid catfish competition on campus for charity. It was never like that when we lived in Nashville.

I was half tempted to schedule a drive-by and just drop in on him one day, soon, but then there was no telling what hell I might walk myself into.

"Mommy, our house is haunted. I don't want to live there anymore," Bryce informed me as the moment I picked him and his brother up from tutoring.

"Yep, Mommy, I heard it too," Byron added.

"You didn't hear it. You were asleep. I tried to wake you up, but you wouldn't get up. I was scared," Bryce said.

I laughed, just imagining him being afraid. "Why didn't you tell your daddy that you were afraid?"

"I tried, but when I called out for Daddy, the ghosts stopped making noise. I heard it again later, and when I called him again, it stopped again. I think the ghosts got scared when I called Daddy. That made them run away."

"Did Daddy come to your room when you called him?"

"No."

"Where was Julie? She didn't come to check on you?" I asked, getting annoyed.

"Julie spent the night at Sandy's house. She went after you left the other night," he answered, unaware of the hell he was unearthing.

"Julie's been gone since I left? What about Brittany?"

"She fixed us some smiley face pancakes that morning after you left. We didn't see her anymore. I asked Daddy if she could come back, but he said you would get mad if she was there."

"Really? What did you have for dinner last night?" My blood boiled.

"We ate some good, good greens, cone-bread, crunchy chicken, and cheese macaroni. It was um-um good," Bryce rushed to answer.

Byron added, "It was super-duper good."

"Did you go to a restaurant?" I asked as nicely as I could.

"No, Daddy cooked it before he picked us up from practice," Byron answered.

I was sure an artery was beating so hard in my head, that it would burst any moment.

"We had brownies too," Byron added.

"Oh yeah, I forgot about that," Bryce confirmed.

I couldn't wait to hear what lie Derrick was going to tell. He couldn't burn toast right without burning the house down, let alone cook a whole meal plus dessert.

"What did you eat the night before?"

"Daddy took us to get some catfish. He said it tastes just like your catfish, but he told the lady that she had the best catfish."

No need to probe that any further. That was quite obvious.

"What did you have for breakfast this morning?"

"Uhm . . . we had oatmeal, banana, orange juice—" Bryce answered.

"And toast with jelly," Byron added.

"Did Daddy fix you all of that by himself?" I don't know why I was torturing myself.

"I guess so. It was on the table when we came downstairs. There wasn't anyone else over," Bryce answered with his naïve innocence.

I knew if I questioned Derrick, he'd turn it all against me for probing.

After some thought, Bryce added, "It tasted like the oatmeal Miss Brittany made for us when you were sick. It was really good."

So was it possible that Brittany prepared meals for them, then Derrick picked the food up and microwaved everything for the kids on his own? Or was Brittany hiding out in my home so my kids wouldn't see her and tell me? But then, who made the toast? Derrick couldn't even do that simple task.

"Did the ghost sound anything like Brittany?" Okay, so I was getting desperate. Sue me!

Byron and Bryce laughed so hard.

"Mommy, stop being silly. Brittany's not a ghost. She'd have to be dead to be a ghost," Bryce said, still amused.

"Wait till I tell Daddy you said Miss Brittany is a ghost."

"Don't . . ." I started to tell him not to say anything, but the more I thought about it, I wanted them to run and tell the whole conversation. Hopefully, I would be right there when they did, so I could see the look on Derrick's face.

Unfortunately, my dear husband didn't make it home before the kids made it to bed. To add insult to injury, somehow Derrick managed to get some laundry done before getting the kids to school and leaving for work. What miracles! (I'm being sarcastic).

The bed had a fresh set of sheets and the bathroom was in perfect order. Perhaps my nose had grown immune to my own scent, but I did smell one of my favorite perfumes on my pillow and his as well. Yep! I was going all the way there, smelling everything.

It's one thing to cheat on me, but in my house and in my bed? I didn't even want to think about it. What would I do if I knew for certain? Just hand my husband over to whomever? Could it have been Carmen there? Would Brittany be so disrespectful to me of all people? Maybe Jocelyn came to get proof that she was with with my husband. What better proof than photos inside my home?

All of these thoughts were making me crazy.

Chapter 15

anelle, what is wrong with you? You have managed to lose two clients in two weeks. I keep telling you that you need to stop with those hormone pills. They're making you mentally unstable," Derrick had the nerve to suggest. "First you're suggesting to our children that Brittany was here in the middle of the night, pretending to be some ghost, then I had Carmen here, simply because I took the kids out for some dinner, that wasn't even at her restaurant. I guess when I picked up the soul food dinner from Alcenia's, I snuck the girls into the bags, huh?" He laughed.

In one fell swoop, Derrick managed to explain away EVERYTHING.

After I left, Brittany hung around to watch the kids, since they forgot to tell me that Derrick went back out after I was on the road, a nervous wreck, thinking my daddy was dying. He was utterly offended that I would even think he would have any other woman in our bed. He suggested that maybe Brittany was in our room going through my perfumes while he was out. It almost sounded plausible. Even worse, he admitted that he swung by "Sister Jocelyn's" with some of the fellas to watch the game and have a few beers.

He said only a fool would tell his wife that he was hanging out at his mistress' house, like that should have been all the proof I needed that there was nothing going on between the two of them. Funny, he never volunteered to tell me that he knew "Sister Jocelyn" outside of church before she mentioned it. Now that she showed me pictures of him hanging out—behaving inappropriately,

I might add—he wanted to talk to me about her as if she was one of the boys. When I asked why he never took me there with him, he said my insecurity was to blame. Supposedly, my insecurity was so embarrassing to him that he couldn't imagine taking my "disrespectful mouth and behavior" to someone's home.

Honestly, if he he had taken me there, yes, I would have a hissy-fit, but he didn't know that for sure. I was surprised to hear he even had any male friends, since I had yet to meet any. Maybe those were guys he met at her house or some strip club he frequented for "business meetings."

I knew one thing—something had to give. I was losing my mind and now my clients. Before the loss of the two, I only had four clients left because of my hectic family schedule since moving to Memphis. At least living in Nashville, I had some help with the kids. Everything fell on my shoulders in Memphis. My ability to concentrate was overshadowed by constant thoughts of my husband being unfaithful. I couldn't understand why he would want us to stay married if he really was doing anything wrong. I thought maybe it was the hormone pills making me crazy. Lord help me if I lost my last two clients and left Derrick to be the sole provider for our family. Then I really wouldn't be able to leave him if I got up the nerve to actually go through with it. I made such horrible mistakes with the clients that I lost, that I couldn't fix my mouth to ask for a reference. They wouldn't even allow me an opportunity to fix my mistakes at no extra cost to them.

I wouldn't mind so much about having so few clients, but they had revenue so low that my fee was probably one of the biggest liabilities on their books. They just didn't really know it because they didn't understand all the numbers stuff like I did. And since I accidentally double-entered all of the checks deposited into their accounts, causing them to overdraw their bank account and bounce payroll checks, I didn't complain when payment was stopped on the check for my services.

Yeah, I was screwing up, big time, but the problem was Derrick, and not so much my pills.

My medical options weren't too great either. If I had a total hysterectomy as suggested by my doctor, I'd still have to take hormone replacement therapy, and I'd need lots of help while I recovered. I had switched hormone pills about four times thus far, due to adverse side effects. I could have had a D&C procedure that might last a couple of months, or I could have done nothing and returned to my previous life of less insane and definitely less paranoid about Derrick cheating on me. Well, I was paranoid before, but was worse with the pills. Even Derrick noticed how much of a problem I was lately.

"You know Julie's sweet sixteen is coming, and we can't afford for you to be messing up now and losing business," Derrick reminded, making me feel worse than before.

"What do you want me to do? I messed up and now I know to be more careful," I snapped.

"Get more clients. You were doing very well with your business. We agreed when we got married that you weren't going to be some stay-at-home mom on the couch watching television all day and getting fat. You kept a full client load even when the kids were babies. What's the problem now? I think turning forty has made you lazy, and keep in mind, a lazy woman is very unattractive to me. I produce winners all day, every day in my line of work. Do you seriously think I want to come home to a loser?"

My dear husband always had a way with words. He knew just the right things to say at just the right times.

"Oh my goodness! And what are you crying about now? Good lord, you cry about everything. Why don't you go put some lingerie on so you can feel better?" he offered as a romantic consolation.

"I don't feel like it," I snapped.

"You're turning me down?" he scoffed. "You're turning me down, Janelle? Do you really want to do that?" he said, getting off of the bed.

I caved. "Fine! I'll go change."

I don't know why I didn't just let him go to the other room to punish me as usual. Honestly, I was feeling so defeated, broken, and confused, I thought a little attention from my husband might be just what my wounded soul needed. What I didn't expect was thoughts of Derrick being replaced by thoughts of Kenny, while my husband attempted to get my mind off of my problems. I was innocently thinking of calling Kenny to see if I might be able to drum up more business, but then the memory of his scent did something to me.

By the time Derrick was done, he was saying, "Wow! We're going to have to do this more often. I don't know what got into you tonight, but I definitely liked it."

In fact, he liked it so much that he woke me up at 4:30am for another round of "it," featuring my carnal, forbidden thoughts of Kenny. For the first time in years, we were scheduled for a sex-lunch date, meaning we'd rendezvous to the house during lunch time for sex.

Unfortunately, Mother Nature showed up that evening, obstructing the promised night of passion we were both looking forward to after the lunch. Derrick got so angry, you would have thought I made it happen. *Sigh.*

Chapter 16

had never been big on sushi, but for whatever reason I was willing to be daring when I met Kenny at the Bluefin for lunch. I kept telling myself that our meeting was strictly business, but the flowers he brought me kind of threw me for a loop. Suddenly, I felt like I was cheating. As he sat across the table from me, I worked hard to push away all of the filthy thoughts, but the hug he greeted me with left his hypnotic scent dancing in my nostrils. *Boy! This is going to be rough.*

Before I could let him know I didn't drink alcohol, he was ordering us something called the Memphis Rita. It was definitely a pretty drink. I hated to have to say I wouldn't drink it, so I decided to just take really small sips to keep from getting drunk. I ended up telling him I didn't drink alcohol, and he apologized and offered to get me something else, but I figured there couldn't be much harm from the one drink.

"How's your business been going since I last saw you?"

I was too embarrassed to tell him about my mess-up, so I told a half-truth. "Please, these people seem to have a hard time making rent, let alone paying my fee. It's time for me to stop doing work for companies without the right revenue."

"I agree. I don't waste my time. However, I'm a little embarrassed now," he said.

"You? Why is that?" I asked, taking a long sip of my sinfully strong drink. It was delicious after the initial kick.

"I have this client I was thinking of pawning off on you. Their revenue is only around fifteen million."

I choked as I was taking another lengthy sip of my drink. No, I was really choking. Drink came from my nose as I attempted to cough. Now I was officially embarrassed. Kenny looked on in horror, unsure of how to help me.

He pulled out his phone (hopefully not to take a picture). "Should I call 9-1-1?"

If Derrick found out about my secret meeting, someone would need to call Jesus himself to help me from the mess I found myself in. I definitely couldn't risk losing a fifteen-million-dollar client over something as stupid as choking to death. Derrick would kill me for that as well.

When I was able to catch my breath, I let Kenny know I would be fine. I excused myself to the ladies' room. The alcohol was kicking in. When I returned to the table, I noticed the drink I had been sipping on was empty. I had a look of dismay on my confused face.

"What's wrong? You'd like another drink? I wasn't sure if I should order it or not since you're not a drinker, but you went through the first one kind of quick, so I wasn't sure."

Aw, he's so thoughtful, I thought, but surely he was be mistaken about me drinking that entire drink. I would never. I only took one or two sips—I think.

Man, he's gorgeous. I wish I could figure out what he's saying.

"I'll just take a water or maybe some coffee," I said when I realized I must have been drunk.

He laughed.

"What's so funny?"

"That's what I just said. Yeah, definitely no more alcohol for you. You should have told me you didn't drink alcohol when I was putting the order in. You didn't have to feel obligated to drink it.

I drank two glasses of water and a cup of coffee to help sober up. I knew Kenny had another meeting scheduled after me, but I felt so special when he cancelled it to make sure I was well. I was feeling a little foolish for causing yet another scene in front of this young man, but when he told me, "You know, one day when we're old and gray, we're going to tell about this day and we are going to laugh so hard, they'll think we'll croak, but today, we just need to make sure you're all right," suddenly I didn't feel so dumb. Actually, for the first time in what seemed like forever, all felt well in the world.

As I sobered up, we continued discussions about his client with the meager fifteen-million-dollar portfolio. He was going to set up a meeting with them for us to go over the clients' needs. He even offered to foot the lunch bill for that meeting, in addition to the one we were somewhat enjoying. I tried desperately to contain my excitement from having a client with a healthy portfolio. I usually get the strugglers— the ones barely able to pay my fees.

Kenny let me know if all went well, he had some other multimillion-dollar portfolios he could turn over to me. I didn't mind having to prove myself to this virtual stranger, who was willing to sacrifice his good name to take a chance on me. Sadly, he seemed to have more faith in me than my own husband. Derrick came into contact with businesses almost daily, and he had yet to throw a bone in my direction. Ever.

I left that meeting on cloud nine. There was nothing anyone could say or do to pop my bubble. When Derrick joked about me having to buy my own flowers in an effort to try to get some attention, I didn't give him the satisfaction of seeing me get upset.

The following day, Derrick came home with a fresh bouquet of flowers and tossed the ones from Kenny. While I should have been happy to receive flowers from Derrick, I was hurt to lose the flowers from Kenny. They made me feel special. However, despite Derrick's all-out attempts to romance me with candles, flowers, and a pair of his new silk boxers, it was Kenny who made love to me . . . in my mind.

Chapter 17

Mom, what's up with your good mood lately?" Julie asked, coming into the kitchen as I fixed dinner. "It's like nothing bothers you anymore."

"You make it sound like a problem or something. You should be happy if I'm in a good mood, shouldn't you?"

"Yeah, I know, but I'm just not used to it. It's almost like waiting for old, cranky, miserable Mom to show back up any moment."

I stared at her for a few minutes to see if she was serious or not. "Gee, thanks," I finally said. "And speaking of my mood, what's your plan for bringing up that history grade? History is simply reading. You're obviously not reading. You've been spending way too much time at Sandy's house and not enough at your own."

"I put her on timeout for a while."

"Timeout? How do you put your best friend on timeout?" I was anxious to hear what occurred between the pair.

"I told her that you've been in a good mood lately and how I was thinking about asking you if I could go to Amber's birthday party, when she opened her stupid mouth and said that you must be in a good mood because Daddy's finally taking care of you right in the bedroom. She made me so angry. How dare she say something so stupid?" Julie said, plopping onto the stool.

I was greatly embarrassed as well as annoyed. The sad part was that she was partly right.

"I really do not like that girl. Why must you hang around with her? She's such a negative influence."

"I think so, sometimes," Julie agreed.

Whoa! A moment for the record books: Julie agreed with something I said.

She continued. "She knew you had that stupid bleeding problem. Why would she think it was something wrong with Daddy?"

"And she knows about my personal—very personal business—how?"

She was working hard to get me out of my good mood, that's for sure.

"I probably told her about it. I know Daddy gets so annoyed with it. He said sometimes he thinks you do it intentionally to make him go away and leave this family. I tried to tell him that you can't help it and he needs to cut you some slack."

Okay, my rage meter was hitting about a seven right now. How dare Derrick have that kind of conversation with our daughter? And then for her to discuss my issues with her friends?

"Julie, please do not be discussing what goes on in this house or with me to your friends. If that's too much to ask, then we'll just have to make sure that time with friends gets eliminated."

"Duh! I'll still see her in school. You can't pick and choose my friends."

"Duh? Oh, I got your 'duh.' How about I put you in public school so you'll have to fight every day instead of learning, and then you'll have no friends?"

"Yeah, right! Like Daddy would actually go for that." She laughed.

"Do you really want to see how low I can go? Your father isn't informed of any of your activities, schooling, friends, or anything else, other than what I tell him."

Julie tried to stare me down. "You wouldn't."

"I would and I will if you keep trying me," I said with a smile. "By the time your father found out, you'd have already experienced your first three beatdowns in public school, all on day-one. Sure, Daddy will get mad and want to switch you back, but with that lengthy waiting list to get into your school, your slot would be gone and you'd have to stay in the public school until Daddy could find you another school, without my help. Now, like I said, try me! Keep telling my business," I dared her.

"I guess the cranky old lady is back!" she shouted as she ran from the kitchen.

When the coast was clear, I laughed so hard. I couldn't wait for her to tell Derrick and then he'd be grumbling about nothing, much like the joy he got from inflicting misery into my life.

Chapter 18

Believe it or not, things were been going pretty well with Derrick and I— plus Kenny. Okay, well, Kenny knew nothing about it, but marital life was good since he had come along. But like any other good thing, eventually it came to an end.

"What is this?" I asked when entering the bedroom to find naked people doing nasty things to each other on our seventy-inch television screen.

Derrick had this big cheesy grin on his face as he laid across the bed in another new pair of silk boxers, looking like he was auditioning for an underwear commercial. He patted the bed in front of him and tried to do this Denzel Washington thing with his lips—or was that LL Cool J?

"Come here baby. It's time for us to try something new. We have to keep the spice going. Plus, I have something for you that I know you're going to enjoy," he said, getting excited before he jumped up from the bed to retrieve a large gift box sitting on the dresser.

I wasn't going along with the pornography, but I was intrigued by the box. I even smiled. I couldn't imagine what would be in a box that size. It was definitely too heavy and large for lingerie.

"Open it!" he said, sounding like an excited parent talking to their kids on Christmas morning.

His level of excitement had me so excited, I sat the box down and decided to show my gratitude with a sensual kiss. It meant a lot to me that my husband was making an effort to repair our damaged marriage. I was so happy, I thought of giving Kenny the night off.

"You haven't even opened the box yet. I can't wait for the reward once you get it open."

"I am just so thankful to have such a beautiful and thoughtful husband. You have no idea how much you mean to me. The fact that you fight so hard for us—for this marriage. You are my everything, Derrick Roberts, but I don't want you to ever feel that we need any filthy porn to keep me loving you with everything inside of me."

He stepped away from me with a combined look of confusion and anger. "You are so ungrateful. Just flat-out ungrateful."

Now I was confused. What did I just do wrong? I thought I was showing my appreciation, saying what his ego needed to hear to be inflated. Woe unto me for trying to be kind.

"I'm sorry. I didn't mean to upset you. I was just letting you know how much I love you. I wanted you to know that before I opened the box, because it doesn't matter what's in the box, my feelings are still the same," I foolishly pleaded to get back into his good graces. I still wasn't watching any porno. Both of our upbringings went against it.

Derrick snatched the box from the bed, where he had placed it for me to open. "You're happy now? There is no gift for you. I don't want you to have it."

"Stop being so childish and give me the box. What's gotten into you?"

"You want the box? You want what's in the box? Here, I'll show you what your ungrateful behind won't be getting. I'm sure I can find someone else to give it to. Someone who will appreciate it."

I stepped back and let him tear open his gift, which obviously wasn't for me in the first place. The more I thought about it, it had to be something inappropriate. The only thing I said controversial that would have set him off this way, was about the pornography. *That must be a box filled with that smut. He's right, he can give that mess to someone else.*

I watched as he ripped the box open, dumping out a plentiful supply of sex objects or toys—I didn't know what to call them. What I did know was that he must have bumped his head if he thought I was supposed to take part in this foolishness.

I can't remember laughing so hard. I actually laughed to tears.

"What's so funny?" he asked with a perplexed look on his face.

When I was able to stop laughing and catch my breath, I simply said, "You . . . this," I said pointing to the objects. "You might as well gather up whatever you need to enjoy your guest bedroom, like every time you get mad at me, because this is a definite no-go."

"I'm not leaving the bedroom tonight, and I suggest you leave if you don't want to watch what's on the screen."

"Not a problem," I said, gathering my bed attire.

He ran and grabbed my arm before I could make it out of the door. "Janelle, Janelle, why are you being so difficult about this? I need to be with my wife tonight." He tried to soften up and rubbed my shoulders.

"I would love to be with my husband, but it won't be with any of that mess," I said, pointing back toward the television and his box of gifts.

He kindly opened the bedroom door. "Goodnight," he rudely said.

"Absolutely. Have fun with your props all by yourself," I said, feeling empowered. I knew that smut would do nothing but heighten his need for sex, so I laughed it off.

However, I wasn't laughing when I climbed onto the bed in the guest room and it smelled like a combination of my perfume, Derrick's cologne, and Brittany's scent. I hadn't slept in the guest room in many months, but I knew I had never worn my perfume while in there. The scent was so nauseating, I got up and stripped the entire bed and replaced everything. The pillow still held the scents, even with the fresh linens, so I opted for no pillow. I most certainly wasn't laughing when Derrick felt the need to crawl his horny behind into bed with me at 3am. I guess his props weren't working out so well for him.

I felt violated and used when he left the room immediately after he was done. I was kicking myself for not standing my ground and allowing myself to be a wastebasket while he pretended I was whatever he was watching.

So what I thought about Kenny? It wasn't the same. No, really, it wasn't.

Chapter 19

Although Pastor Hill was college educated, Mother Hill only went as far as the third grade in school. She married Pastor Hill when she was just thirteen years old and he was twenty-two. She was one of seventeen children, so her parents were happy to marry her off to the highest bidder. I guess that was something common back in her day.

I can't imagine what the draw was for them, but twelve kids and fifty-eight years later, they were still together. Pastor Hill started preaching when he was only twenty years old—do the math. He was already a preacher when he took a child for a bride. But I ain't passing any judgment or anything.

Somehow, an uneducated woman managed to raise a dozen college educated children. Hats off to her for that alone. Now, although they had college degrees, that didn't mean they were successful in their lives. Out of the twelve, only three went on to prosperous careers. Well, I didn't count Minister Hill, who is the eldest son and set to take over the church. He just had "perverted crook" coming from his pores. He lived a lavish lifestyle, but he hardly worked for it. I think he was a glorified prostitute. He was always providing private prayer to the lonely widows, and the church became beneficiary to large donations. But I ain't passing any judgment or anything.

Another of the sons was head of the Deacon Board. That was his only job. Another perverted crook. You would think with five daughters, one of them could have been the church secretary. Nope, that would be too much like right.

Instead, they had some tight-bodied, thirty-year-old girl who never finished school. There were a few women who headed up some of the many ministries, and they were all youthful and perky looking. I couldn't help but wonder what the requirements were to get a position at our church.

Sometimes—most of the times—I felt like our church was one great big orgy. Derrick, being the man of the house, chose that church for our family. He liked that Pastor Hill had been preaching for sixty years and was married to the same woman. The church was recommended to him by one of his colleagues, supposedly. I say, "supposedly" because as long as we attended, I had yet to meet the colleague.

Sadly, I was unable to make any friends of my own at the church, or anywhere for that matter. Mother Hill was the only person I felt that I could talk to. Yes, holding an intelligible conversation with her was a great challenge, but it was almost like being in a foreign country—eventually you learn the language of the natives. It's a shame no one ever taught Mother Hill to speak correctly. One of her daughters was a teacher and surely could have compassionate enough to help her own mother. But I ain't passing any judgment or anything.

With things taking an ugly turn at home, I set up an appointment to speak with Mother Hill. I really didn't know where else to turn. I didn't dare talk to any of the other women ministers in the church. They were all personally ordained and trained by Pastor Hill. Not passing judgment or anything, but that sure didn't mean that they were qualified to minister to the people. To the Pastor maybe, but not the congregation. Definitely not to me.

I met Mother Hill at her beautiful mansion for the first time. Her butler showed me to her den, where she awaited my arrival. Shoot! I guess she figured that she had it going on and didn't need to learn to read, write, speak, or anything else for anyone.

"Thank you for taking the time to speak with me today, Mother Hill. I truly appreciate this blessing," I said. I gave her a big hug while she remained seated in what probably was her favorite sitting chair. She sat like royalty. I felt like an unworthy peasant in her presence, as I stood waiting for her to offer me to sit. I guess she'd never heard of manners, either.

"Wha' ya dandin der fo? Sat yursef down!" she scolded.

I smiled as I took the seat nearest to her.

"Wha' ya need, daughter? Wha' brings ya ta see me?"

She seemed irritated. I was scared to talk about my own problems. I thought of just saying, "Never mind." I took a deep breath and just let it out.

"My husband wants to start using filthy movies and objects in our bedroom and I'm not comfortable with any of it. Things have not been going too well for us lately, and I'm not sure what to do. I feel like my marriage is coming to an end and I don't know how I'll get along if that happens," I said, letting the stream of tears fall from my eyes.

Mother Hill grabbed the box of tissues on her end table and gave it to me.

"Thank you," I said after I collected a couple of tissues from the box.

"Da Bible say, ya gotta do wha' yo husband say. If dat be wha' he won', den dat be wha' cha give 'em," she snapped.

I sat for a moment trying to recall where in the Bible it said that, and how she would possibly know what any bible would say. I thought about calling her on her words, but then she said, "Look at Ephesians five. It tell ya ta obey dat man, an' let 'em have his way."

Lord help me! I should have known that would have been programmed into her thinking by her husband. Surely, Paul didn't mean for there to be vile things introduced into the bedroom when he wrote the book of Ephesians. In the same chapter, it is written about the whoremonger, filthiness, and uncleanliness, all which perfectly seemed to describe Derrick at this point. But I didn't dare debate with Mother Hill. After all, it was me who sought her counsel. I just never thought it would be so warped . . . or maybe I was truly the wrong one on this matter.

"Wha'! Ya don' ba'leaf me? Look it up an' see fo yo'sef. I mights not kno' mush, but I kno' da word fo myself."

But how? How do you know, Mother Hill? I so desperately wanted to ask.

"Thank you so much for your wonderful words of wisdom, Mother Hill. I knew I did right coming here for wisdom." I smiled, although I felt it had to be the greatest lie I'd ever told.

"Try reaching yur Bible sometime," she briskly responded.

It took a second for me to process that her "reaching" meant "reading."

"Yes, yes, you are correct. I definitely need to get more Bible reading done." I was about to jump up to leave, but Mother Hill's unusually abrasive demeanor with me was bothering me. So I asked, "Mother Hill, I have to ask, is everything okay? You don't quite seem yourself today."

Now it was Mother Hill pulling tissues from her box. She was crying. I immediately jumped up to console her.

"Oh my goodness, Mother Hill! What's wrong. Are you feeling all right"

She allowed me to hug her for a few seconds before pushing me away. She motioned for me to return to my seat, as she continued to wipe her eyes and nose. I sat patiently until she was ready.

"Brit'ny's wit chile. I think she been wit someone husband, but she swear it be Brother Fredrick's boy, Danny."

I covered my mouth. I was shocked by Mother Hill's accusation of her granddaughter being with someone's husband. I was also shocked that she called out Julie's crush, Danny. Julie would be devastated to think that Danny was intimately involved with Brittany, whom she already doesn't seem to like. But for Brittany to be pregnant by Danny would send Julie over the edge. Although we didn't permit Julie to date, I still made it a point to violate her diary every once in a while, and I knew Danny took up a lot of those pages. I was also shocked because Danny was at least a year younger than Brittany. He was still in high school.

But then I remembered when she mentioned to me that she knew who the father was.

Mother Hill continued. "I don' know wha ta do 'bout dat chile. Ha min' is messed up. She don' care 'bout nuttin' or nobody but ha'self. She dun broke up good fam'lies wit ha' foolishness. She selfish."

"But maybe she's telling the truth about the baby belonging to Danny. He's so young. Too young to be a father, but at least he's no one's husband," I said, hoping to make her feel better.

"Brother Fredrick say his boy a virgin. He ain' been wit no girl. Brit'ny say he a lie. I think *she* a lie. She ain' gon' tell me who husband got ha' knocked up. She the Devil. I tell ya!"

Wow! That's sad and scary.

"Well, whoever he is, I hope he doesn't attend our church. That would truly be a tragedy."

"I sho' he a no-good devil too, sat right der. Prob'ly been to our home and ate at our table wit us. Dat why I tell you don' let no Juss-a-bel get in yo home or yo marriage," she warned. "Ya jus' neva know who da Devil be."

I frowned at her words. I had the "She-devil" all up in my house and around my husband. I suddenly thought back on Brittany's words about how Derrick would die if she were pregnant, but she said it was because he was helping her get into school. Derrick was thirty years older than Brittany, and I just *knew* he would know better than to get involved with our babysitter. But it's not like married men haven't been known to do something so reprehensible. The thought of them even looking at the other's private parts made me want to kill them both.

Rage started filling me. I couldn't help but ask, "Mother Hill, you don't think she'd go after my husband, do you? Would she stoop that low to betray my trust?"

"She da Devil! Don' trust no devil. But ya need to ask if ya da one leavin' room fo da Devil ta git in yo marriage."

Oh lord! I'd left a revolving door open in my marriage. Doors, windows— everything. When Derrick tried to get me to know Carmen and the other Jezebels, I absolutely refused. I should have been keeping my enemies close and not allow my husband to sneak off behind my back to see them.

I thought back to three occasions when Brittany was left alone in my home with Derrick. Could they? Would he? I thought about Derrick buckling down on our date nights since Brittany started babysitting. But then that didn't make sense, because she even tried to help him be more romantic, and I'd be home with the kids for the most part.

As I tried to shake the thoughts from my head, I abruptly jumped up and told Mother Hill I had to leave. I needed to get to a calendar to see the times Brittany was left alone with Derrick. I also needed to strategize on how to seal the cracks in my marriage or be prepared to let my family go. And I would not be letting my family go without a fight, especially when I had a husband fighting for our family. I was going to make sure Brittany has no more direct contact with Derrick. No more car rides or anything without me or the kids present. But of course, I couldn't let on about my suspicions to Derrick, because he'd again tell me how ridiculously insecure I was being. I definitely needed to work on finding a new babysitter. Someone old and wrinkly with trifocals and white hair. Yep! That'd be the perfect babysitter. No more of those young, sexy girls.

Chapter 20

Did you hear? Brittany's having a baby. You're going to have to find a new babysitter for the brats," Julie said to me while I sat trying to read my book in peace.

Derrick had one of his late meetings *again*, and I was trying to keep from going crazy with thoughts of Brittany possibly seducing my husband in my home. Out of insecurity, I did call to "check up on" Brittany, when Derrick let me know he wouldn't make it home for dinner. I needed to make sure he was not with Brittany. Thankfully, they weren't together. I was able to hear Mother Hill fussing in her own unique dialect in the background. That helped ease my anxieties. That was, until my darling daughter felt the need to interrupt my peace and bring Brittany back to the forefront of my mind.

"Yes, I heard. I understand that Danny is the father," I answered.

"That's a lie!" Julie yelled. She looked as if she'd be ready to fight me if I dared to accuse her crush of being interested in the likes of Brittany. "He is not interested in being with that walking disease."

"Julie! Watch your mouth and tone."

"I'm just saying, he's not interested in her." Julie handed me her tablet opened to her Facebook page, which I forbade but her father allowed.

"What is this?" I asked, unsure of what I was supposed to be seeing. I saw the page of someone with a rainbow flag for their profile picture, and the username "Musik IsMyLife."

"That's Danny's Facebook page. Look at what he posted about an hour ago. He even changed his profile picture."

I looked for the post from an hour ago and found:

> I see I am being forced to come out of my closet today. This whack girl from my church, who sleeps with everybody, is pregnant and lying to everyone, saying it's my baby. I don't know why she chose me to pin her dirty deeds on, but I can assure all of you in FB Land that Musik IsMyLife is NOT the father. I have never been with a girl in my life. I am not even attracted to any. I am, however, attracted to my own kind. Even Stevie Wonder could see that I would NEVER be interested in the likes of Brittany.
>
> Girl, you better go find your baby-daddy, but I ain't it. And everyone in our church knows that her crusty butt only goes after old married men who give her money and gifts. I'm only seventeen, so I definitely don't fit the profile, although I did hear she'll help break a young boy's virginity. Don't they have laws against people like her? She should have known better than to try to come for me, because I know it all and I'll tell it all. Don't try to smear my good name. Contrary to popular belief, I got a man! (followed by a tag and a #DropsMic)

There were over 150 comments on that post. Many were "LOL," but several of them were publicly shaming Brittany by sharing some of their deeds with her. However, I did note the one comment from "Brittany AppleBottom," showing off a photo of her clothed behind, saying, "Dude, get your life! You just mad I didn't want you. I'd turn gay too if I was rejected by me. Believe it or not, I do have some standards, and you certainly fall below them."

Underneath her comment, there were at least fifty guys directly responding with, "I had you!"

I wanted to cry for Brittany. That type of public humiliation, on top of everything else the child had been through, was totally uncalled for. But then again, there was the mystery of why Brittany would name Danny as the father when there were at least fifty or more other guys standing up to admit that they'd been with her. Why not pin the baby on one of them?

I guess I was starting to understand why Mother Hill was so convinced that the father must be some married man. She had plenty of single boys to blame, but she chose the one she'd never been with, who was now outing himself to the world. I couldn't imagine how his parents were reacting to the news either way. It must not have been great to cause Danny to take to such a public forum to denigrate Brittany's character.

"Isn't this the boy you've had a crush on since we've moved to Memphis?" I asked Julie as I handed her back her tablet.

"Who told you that? Were you reading my diary or something?"

Oops!

"No," I answered as if offended. "You don't think I hear you and Sandy talking about your crushes? Why would I read your diary? That's such an invasion of privacy." I had to add on the last line for good measure.

"Oh. Oh yeah," she answered, embarrassed. "I am so bummed right now. I need to call someone.

"Well, I'm here if you'd like to talk," I said, trying to soothe her disappointment.

"Uh, NOT! You're my mom. I can't talk to you about stuff like this. I only told you so you could get a new babysitter, since Brittany obviously will be busy with her own baby. Eew! What kind of fool would get her pregnant? She never heard of birth control?"

Well, I was glad my child heard at least something I said during one of our many discussions . . . about birth control.

I could hardly concentrate on my book after Julie returned to her room to gossip on the phone. My feelings about Brittany were all over the place. In one sense, I wanted to help her, and in another I didn't trust her. She needed someone like me who could be mother-like and give her guidance and career direction. She needed to learn boundaries and what love really was. I really felt like I could get through to her.

Chapter 21

knew I was supposed to be taking measures to close the gaps to the infiltrations of my marriage, but for some reason or another, I felt a need to spruce up my appearance for my meeting with Kenny. It was the least I could do, being the man was mentally in my marital bed more times than I could count. At least I didn't call my husband by another man's name as my husband had so insensitively done to me.

Derrick had to take one of his last-minute business trips, to Chicago this time. I was glad I didn't have to worry about him seeing my DKNY pencil skirt hugging my hips just right, my Christian Louboutins adding depth to my calves, my plunging neckline in my Jason Wu blouse, or the sassy Armani animal-textured blazer that brought it all together, giving the appearance of subtle freak, yet professional. Yeah, Derrick would have died if he had seen me. I brought along a neck scarf just in case I didn't have enough time to make it home to change before I picked up the kids. I would hate for word to get back to him about my exposition of cleavage. I just needed to feel sexy today. I needed someone to take notice for a change, instead of feeling like the invisible wife and mother.

When I arrived at the restaurant, Kenny was already seated, but he stood up with a "Wow!" look on his face when he saw me approaching. My head was so big in that moment, you couldn't tell me a thing.

"Well, look at you looking all fine and fabulous. You look like you just stepped off of a page from *Vogue* magazine. And I love, love, love that shade of lipstick on you. Girl, you know you are owning this place; got every man turning his head to take a look at you."

This was just what my poor ego needed. He made me feel so good, I wanted to kiss him, especially when he lifted the bouquet of flowers from the empty seat next to his and said, "A little something special for the lady." I did give him a hug, and even that had me feeling all tingly when his hardwood cologne scent tickled my nostrils. I may have even held him a bit longer than I should have. When I was seated, the server came over to get my drink order. No alcohol this time.

"I have some good news for you," he said with a huge smile.

"Great! I could definitely use some," I said, fighting to stay in my moment of feeling like a million dollars.

"Oh, what's wrong? Anything you want to talk about? You know, I'd like to think of myself as a friend. I know our lunches have been about business, but I'm here if you ever just want to get stuff off your chest." In that moment, he looked at my chest, causing the girls to come to attention. He added, "I have to admit, you are really killing it today. I'm surprised your husband let you out of the house this morning."

I blushed. "Thank you, and to be honest, my husband is away on a business trip to Chicago. He hates when I experiment with different lip or eye colors."

"You are wearing that purple makeup like it's nobody's business, and even got the matching nails. Trust me, I don't think everyone could pull it off. It definitely works with your outfit."

"Thank you," I repeated. "So what's the great news?"

"Two more clients. One has a portfolio of thirty-six million, and the other is only thirty million dollars. You think you can handle it?"

I sat stunned. Kenny was GIVING me these clients that he could be getting paid off of. I couldn't ever remember anyone doing something so spectacular for me. For a hot second, I felt like I might have been in love with Kenny.

He was every woman's dream—charismatic, thoughtful, handsome, even sexy. *Whew!* It suddenly got hot.

"Kenny, I don't know what to say. This is wonderful."

"Oh, and I bumped your fee up as well, so they know to pay you $550 per hour, and any collections will be on a percentage basis."

I almost choked again. I definitely gasped.

He continued. "I couldn't believe you only charged the other client $125 per hour. I wanted to strangle you when I heard about it. We don't do discounts. You need to be dressing like you are right now all the time—designer head to toe. Target is good for milk, bread, and a toothbrush. NOT for where we get our clothes from." He chuckled.

If I could even earn over $2,500 for a mere five hours of work, per day, I'd definitely be in designers all day, every day. Truth is, I felt guilty for charging the first client $125 per hour, whereas I was only charging my other clients between $30 and $75 per hour. Now I knew better.

"Wow, Kenny! I can't believe you are being so generous to me." I stood up to give him another hug. I was so happy I wanted to cry, but I was so tired of crying over every little thing.

"Okay, so it's friend time," he said, immediately taking his seat. "What's got you all bummed?"

I shared the story of Brittany with him and how I'd been struggling with the thought of helping her or turning away from her.

"I could see how a compassionate, sensitive woman like you would be torn. Me and everyone else in the world would say run away with the quickness, but I don't know, you might be able to get through to her like no one else can. Maybe she's like that because no one gives her positive attention. You say she brags about her derrière all the time. Seems that's the only attention she knows. On the other hand, I don't think I'd want her around my husband, and he's gay." Kenny laughed, as his words stunned the literal hell out of me. "Speaking of babies, my partner and I are expecting our child in another four months. We are so excited."

"Huh?" was all I could say.

"Yeah, we paid a surrogate and used my sperm, so he or she will be my own child."

"Huh?" I repeated, still shocked. Let me see if I got this right: the man that I have been lusting over has a husband—gusband or whatever they call them? Suddenly I felt ashamed as a draft reminded me that my cleavage was intentionally exposed for this man and he's married to a man? Oh, what luck! In that moment, I was understanding how Julie felt to learn that her longtime crush was also gay.

I burst out into laughter. He looked confused.

"Did I say something funny?" he asked.

"If I told you, you wouldn't believe it," I answered.

In that same split second, my laughter came to an abrupt halt as I watched my husband exiting the same restaurant with his hand so low on some woman's back. Only a fool would think they hadn't slept together. Even worse, from what I could see, she was beautiful—professional appearance and classy. It's no wonder Derrick didn't spot me when I came in; he was too enthralled with her.

I bawled up and cried like Lucy, from an episode of *I Love Lucy*. Kenny looked both embarrassed and concerned.

"Janelle, what's wrong? What happened?" he asked trying to console me.

"Derrick!" I said.

"Huh? Derrick?"

"My husband. He just left this restaurant with a beautiful woman," I said before sobbing some more. I bet my makeup wasn't cute anymore.

"Didn't you say he was in Chicago? You must have been mistaken."

"Trust me, I'd know my husband if he were standing in a stadium full of lookalikes." Anger was setting in.

"Well, that definitely must have been him," Kenny chuckled. "Do you think he saw you over here?"

"I doubt it. I didn't notice him until they got to the exit and he turned to get a toothpick and mints from the hostess station."

"Wow! Janelle, I'm so sorry to hear. At first you're concerned about the babysitter and now this. So not cool. But you know what you're going to do?"

"What's that?" I asked, digging into my purse for a mirror to assess the damage.

"You are going to march into that ladies' room and get that beautiful face of yours tidied up a bit, and then you are going to come back here and focus on the gobs of money you're going to start making to keep you looking fleek at all times from here on out."

"Looking who? Fleek? What's that?

Yeah, I was feeling old. My slang terminology was a bit weak and dated.

"Fleek is on point. Fierce!" he answered with a smile. "You're going to make your husband have second thoughts about stepping out on you. And if he chooses that path, then you'll be financially straight for yourself. You just have to keep it together. Serve your clients well, make those coins, and be the boss of your own life."

Dang! I was in love with Kenny! He was just the man I needed.

When I returned from the ladies' room, I decided to come clean about my lusting. I figured it was safe to do so since he was officially off limits, although he should have been off limits for the simple fact that I was married. We had a good laugh. Felt good having a friend.

When I arrived home later that evening, Derrick was home, changed into some relaxed attire, and working on his laptop. I was soooo glad I pulled my neck scarf out before I picked up the kids.

"Wow! Baby, you look great!" he said with a huge grin. "A business meeting?"

My poor emotions were all over the place. I was thrilled for the compliment from my husband. I was happy to find him home and not someplace lying about being away in Chicago. But then I was still concerned about the woman I saw him with.

"Yes, yes. I picked up two new clients today. I'm so excited about that. I thought you were still in Chicago." I tried to casually mention as he actually got up and greeted me with a hug and then a kiss.

My heart was in my throat as I was still able to smell Kenny's cologne on my jacket. Surely, Derrick would smell it. I was glad I left the flowers in my trunk.

"That trip was a waste of time and energy. I was on a flight back this morning, arranged a business meeting for lunch, and came straight home. Thought I might surprise you. Figured we could take the kids out for dinner tonight. Maybe some pizza or something casual. I know we never do anything together anymore."

Okay, who is this, and what have they done with my husband?

"Sounds great! Let me go change into something comfortable. You can let the kids know."

Before I could pull away to head upstairs, he pulled me back to passionately kiss me.

Okay, really, who is this man?

As I headed up the stairs, his eyes followed me. "Sexy! Just pure sexiness!"

I felt like I floated the rest of the way.

The night ended perfectly. Not a single hiccup or flaw. I didn't even need Kenny in the bedroom that night. I don't know who the woman was and didn't bother to ask since everything was going so well. It seemed pointless.

Chapter 22

With Julie's sweet sixteen event getting closer, it also meant more conversation with my mom to keep her abreast of all the costs. I chose not to tell her or Derrick about my new salary. Figured that was a need-to-know basis, and for the sake of Julie's over-the-top party, no one needed to know. Otherwise, they'd try to spend that right from under me for the Queen of Brat's party.

With each conversation, Momma asked about Derrick and my marriage, yet she was the main one always telling me to stop talking about what goes on in my marriage. Typically, I didn't tell her much, because it was almost sure to get back to Janae. However, since the day in the restaurant with Kenny, I'd been troubled about whether or not to inquire about who the woman was. Everything had been going well at home for a change. I didn't want to rock the boat, but not knowing who she was, was killing me. So I asked Momma, "Momma, if you saw Daddy out with another woman, would you say something or would you keep it to yourself?"

"It depends on what good you think would come from it," she answered.

"What good would come from it?" I repeated. "How could there possibly be anything good that comes from it?

"Well, I guess you just answered your own question then—with a question at that." She laughed.

I wasn't the least bit amused.

"When I spoke with Mother Hill from my church, she said I need to stop letting others infiltrate my marriage, but my friend says I should just leave it alone and focus on myself."

"And what did your husband have to say when you told him that you go around talking to everyone about your marriage? How did he take that?"

I pouted. I was glad she couldn't see me. I was rolling my eyes as well.

She continued. "I know you're sitting over there rolling your eyes, pouting, but your paranoia will be the death of your marriage."

"It's not paranoia. I saw him in the restaurant with his hand, inappropriately, too low on the woman's waist. His hand should not be touching any woman the way I saw him."

"Good lord, child! Stop with the nonsense. Who does that man come home to every night? Who does he generously provide for? Nothing else should matter!"

"But that's just it; he doesn't come home to me every night. Ironically, the day I saw him, he told me that he was away on a business trip in Chicago. I haven't seen one receipt or airline ticket that shows he was in Chicago."

"Maybe he turned the receipts in to his job. It was a business trip, right?"

I hated when she was right.

"There have been times he takes these trips and I'll see receipts and other times, I see no receipts."

"Janelle, you look for trouble, you're sure to find it. Stop looking for something wrong. I just spoke with him the other day, and he says everything is great. That's what you should be saying when someone asks you."

"It's probably great for him because he's the one doing the cheating. It's not great for the one being cheated on," I said, more frustrated than before. I know I should have just left well enough alone, but I just had to pick a battle with Momma.

"Let me ask you this: While he was leaving the restaurant with a woman, who—and yes I said *who*—were you sitting there with that you couldn't go and let him know you too were there?"

"I was there on business, Mom. I didn't want to cause a scene, just in case."

That was mostly true. Honestly, had I been with there my cleavage exposed with anyone other than a gorgeous Kenny, I would have surely made my way to that exit to stop him before he left. Even for business.

"Janelle, hush up that tale! Why didn't you simply excuse yourself and tell them you needed to speak with your husband? You didn't because you were sitting there, too busy with your own forbidden lunch date. You think I haven't been on this earth longer than you have? I know you, and I know you were up to no good, or else you would have let your husband know you were there. Now, I'm going to say this just once, you better end that affair you have going on, because that will destroy your family."

"Me! Affair?! What affair?" I was shocked. So what my lunch date was initially questionable, but how dare my own mother accuse me of the affair and not Derrick? I couldn't take any more. "Bye, Mom! I have to go now. I have work to do. You know, for my business that you seem to forget I have."

My mother laughed. "Girl, bye! Be silly if you want to."

"Silly?" I yelled through the phone.

Again she said, "Bye!" and then ended the call.

I was hot!

Momma had me so annoyed, I was biting everyone head off that evening. Derrick started accusing me of going crazy from the hormone pills again, and that was enough to make him opt to sleep in the guest bedroom that night.

Chapter 23

At least Derrick was considerate enough to let his parents know that he would be absent for the second time for our Fourth Sunday family dinner. They also opted to skip dinner, which was the opening of a Pandora's Box, meaning no mincing of words. No filters.

"I don't understand what could keep Derrick away from the family for the second time," my dad said while we were all set at the table. "It just don't feel like family without Derrick, Paul, and Erma. At least Paul and Erma could have come. They don't have to stay away just because Derrick don't show. What could be more important than sitting down with your family once a month?"

"Oh, John. I'm sure they'll be here next time," Momma answered.

"You know his job has him working like crazy," JJ said in Derrick's defense.

Janae slammed her hand on the table, startling everyone. "Bull!"

"Watch your language," Daddy scolded.

"And your tone," Momma added.

"I just can't take any more of the foolishness. I think I'm going to stop coming here as well. I can't believe the insanity I have allowed myself to sit through each month. Everyone at this table, from the youngest to the oldest, knows that selfish pig is out rendezvousing with his mistress. He's not here because he's too busy boning all the women Janelle know about, but won't put a stop to, because she's too scared she might disappoint these brats if she divorces the old lying bastard," Janae stood up to announce.

We all sat with our mouths wide open. I couldn't believe Janae would stoop so low, especially in front of my three children.

"What's boning?" Byron asked.

"You kids go eat in the kitchen," Momma ordered.

"I want to stay and hear about Daddy," Bryce objected. "I want to know what that is too."

"Julie, take your brothers and go to the kitchen," Momma said again.

Tears poured from Julie's eyes. "This is all your fault!" she directed her words to me. "You can't ever do anything right. I think I need to just kill myself so I won't be as stupid as you are. Daddy said you are so insecure that you're even jealous of your own daughter," she yelled, foaming at the mouth while tears poured. "You're pathetic!"

"Julie!" Daddy snapped.

"Janelle, you're going to just let your child speak to you like that? You need to smack the crap out of her. That's why she treats you like that," Janae scolded.

"I still wanna know what boning is," Bryce asked again.

"Get your plate and get on to that kitchen like you were told!" Daddy yelled.

The boys quickly did as instructed. Julie sat with her arms folded, staring me down, as if she wanted to fight. Me? I did what I do best. I cried.

"Julie, you want us all to give you this grand birthday celebration, yet you're sitting here disrespecting your mother and defying your grandparents. I'm not having it. Keep it up!" JJ said sternly. I couldn't even believe the creep had my back. He was the main one luring my husband to other women.

"'Cause she's just a big brat. She always expects to have her way, and she's totally disrespectful to everyone, except that cheating toad. And why would that donkey be telling her that her mother is jealous of her? That's way out of line," Janae said. "Let her keep sitting here. I'll go into the kitchen. I don't even want to be in the same room with her. She's a miserable brat. And Janelle, you'd be a bigger fool to give her that party." Janae picked up her plate and went to the kitchen. Undoubtedly, she'd explain what boning is to Byron and Bryce.

"You're so stupid that you just sit there crying and let your sister be mean to me. You're weak and spineless, just like Daddy says you are."

"Julie, don't you speak to your mother like that, ever again!" Daddy yelled. I thought he was about to get up and charge at Julie, he was so angry.

Julie jumped up from the table, causing her chair to fall over. "Fine, I'll just go kill myself then!" She ran upstairs and slammed a door.

"Lil Sis, you really need to handle that girl," my brother said, agreeing with my sister. "She shouldn't be talking to you in that manner. I know for a fact that Derrick would never say any of that foolishness to that child, because he adores his wife."

"She really shouldn't be talking that way," my mother added, ganging up on me. "Let me go upstairs and make sure she's all right. I hate that she has to suffer like this." She got up to go see about my victimized daughter.

I was ready to kill myself when Bryce appeared from the kitchen and asked, "Mommy, Daddy is putting his ding-ding in another lady? We're going to have two mommies now?"

JJ burst out laughing then said, "Nah, little man. Your Aunt Janae is a nut. You're not going to have any more mommies. You only get one."

"Aunt Janae said Daddy's going to leave us and go find some other mommies to put his ding-ding in," Bryce said before crying.

"Janae!" Daddy yelled. "Get your tail out here, NOW!"

Janae came from the kitchen laughing, with Byron on her heels.

"What's wrong with you, girl?" Daddy asked.

"What? These kids deserve the truth. They think he's some god while he treats our sister and your daughter like doo-doo. The devil needs to be exposed. I can't stand how he treats Janelle. She's like a Stepford Wife. Ask her when's the last time she had any recreation. She can't say, because she's had none since she's been with the creep. But this is yours and mom's fault for making her believe she has to put up with the nonsense just to stay married. She's being tortured. Look at her. Do you really think she's happy with her husband, especially when his phone is loaded with photos of naked women's private parts?"

JJ laughed. "That doesn't mean he's doing the nasty with anyone else. When he comes to the A-T-L, we hang out and check out women, but he never crosses the line. He lets everyone know he's married and loves his wife only."

Janae looked at JJ before saying, "Do you know how stupid you sound?"

"Daddy got pictures of naked girls on his phone?" Bryce asked, reminding us all that they were in the dining room.

"Get your butt back in that kitchen!" Daddy yelled again, scaring them both away.

"Dad used to do stuff too and had pictures of women as well," JJ added. "He and Momma are still together, and she's not all bent out of shape. Janelle doesn't have a problem with her husband until you start butting your nose into their business."

I was finally ready to speak up for myself. As much as I couldn't stand Janae for always starting the mess, she always seemed to have my back. "Actually, JJ, no—I am not okay with what's going on, and I think it's even more despicable for my own brother to be taking my husband out to check out other women. Infidelity begins with the lusting, but you wouldn't know anything about infidelity because you've always been too much of a whore to marry anyone."

"Dag! I call myself trying to do you a favor by keeping up with what he's doing and trying to make him comfortable enough to talk to me. If I think he's out of order, I do let him know," JJ said, seeming offended.

"You are a piece of work, JJ. Don't have me cussing you out here in Daddy's house," Janae said. "How do you think taking a man away from his wife and children to go see naked women is supposed to be helpful? He might not be thinking about other women if you weren't always making the weak turd come out with you."

"Well, do you think it's okay for your sister to be involved with another man?" Daddy asked, shocking us all. "Yeah, Janelle, your momma told me you seeing some other man and was in the restaurant with him when you saw Derrick, but was too scared to let him know you were there. That ain't right! The Bible says two wrongs don't make it right."

Oh lord. Here we go with the Bible misquotes.

I was too stunned to speak. I couldn't believe Momma would tell Daddy I was cheating on my husband, or that Daddy would think Derrick's actions were justifiable even if I really were cheating.

"Go 'head, girl!" Janae shouted with excitement. "You do you. Get your groove however you gotta."

"That ain't right, Sis. At least Derrick didn't sleep with them. You taking this way too far now. What if Momma cheated on Daddy? We'd be all messed up. That's selfish."

I opened my mouth to speak a couple of times but couldn't get the words out. After a few tries, I finally said, "How dare you? You of all people, and you too?" I said first to JJ and then to Daddy. "First of all, Momma had no business telling you that lie, because I have never cheated nor attempted to cheat on my husband. I have a business and I have clients. The day I saw Derrick in that restaurant with another woman, I was sitting with a married, gay man, who was providing me with multimillion-dollar clients. I wasn't about to blow my business deal for some ugly confrontation—for something that may have been innocent."

"Girl, please! You know there was nothing innocent about his being there with another woman. But I don't blame you for not sacrificing your business deal for that loser. You better stack up your paper. You never know when you might have to fly solo."

I agreed with Janae's words. I didn't believe there was anything innocent about it. I didn't mean to let everyone know I was making good money now, but my back was against the wall. Nonetheless, they still didn't really know how much.

"Janelle, this is why you always have problems, because you're always telling everyone all of your business," my mother fussed, coming into the dining room. "Did you tell how you told the man all of your marital business? And what you doing messing with a gay man who's married? Surely, you know better than that."

I couldn't take it anymore. I got up from the table, called for my kids, and said, "It's time to go."

They were all excited to be gone from that atrocity. However, upon arrival at home, the boys wasted no time letting Derrick know that they knew he was putting his ding-ding inside of other girls. Of course, that was my fault as well. Yep! I had to be punished, so he stayed out for the night while I cried endlessly. Ending my own life even crossed my mind a time or two. Thankfully, God saved me from my own foolish thoughts, and I fell asleep.

Chapter 24

Things had been very tense in our home for about a week. Derrick would barely acknowledge me, but he was still kind to the kids when he was around them for the few minutes he was home before going to bed. His job, you know.

I was surprised when he called and told me to have Julie dressed up for a father-daughter date. He said to make sure she was elegantly dressed and he would pick her up that following evening like a real date. I went through the trouble of getting her a dress, getting her hair done, having her nails perfectly manicured for her outfit, and I even helped her with a light application of makeup. I won't lie; it felt good spending this time with my wayward daughter.

Derrick rang the bell at 6 p.m. as scheduled and greeted Julie with flowers and a kiss to her cheek. The gesture made me remember why I loved him so much. He dropped her off at 9:30. I thought for sure he was playing the part, since he didn't come in the house.

Julie twirled around, happy as if she'd just found love.

"Where's your dad?" I asked when half an hour had gone by and Derrick still hadn't come into the house.

"Oh, he left. He said he had some work left at the office that he needed to get done."

I was put off by that. It was a Saturday night. "Oh?" I asked.

"Mom, I have the greatest dad in the world. We should make an award for him."

I laughed. I wondered what award I'd ever get.

"I'm glad you enjoyed yourself. Where'd you go?"

"Daddy took me to a dance at his job. I was the only kid there. Everyone was all dressed up, but when we danced, Daddy did our kind of dances, and everyone gathered around in a circle to watch us. It was so cool. Then he took me to his office to show me where he works. His office is huge. He has a big desk and chair. He looked like a king in it. He has a nice leather sofa in there and tons of books on the shelves going all the way up to the ceiling."

As Julie spoke with excitement, I tried to maintain a smile as the wheels turned inside my head. *Why didn't I know anything about this dance, nor was I invited? How come I've never seen his huge office?*

I was feeling a combination of anger and jealousy. If I dared to let my anger show, I knew I'd never hear the end of it—my jealousy and insecurity toward my own daughter. Actually, I felt jealous because Derrick didn't think enough of me to invite me to such an important function. I would have loved to put on my elegant attire and get dolled up for a change. I was hurt. Maybe that was his intention: to inflict pain.

Julie went on and on. I mostly tuned her out, but I managed to catch her question: "Why would you be trying to divorce a man like Daddy? He is the best father in the world."

"Huh?" I asked. I was confused. "Divorce? Where'd you get that idea?"

"Daddy. He said you want to get divorced and that's why you won't try fun things to stay married. I told him I'd talk to you. He really wants to stay married and keep his family, Mom."

I was taken aback. How dare he discuss our private matters with our child! To Julie and Derrick, I would have been completely out of line if I tried to defend myself or voiced my disappointment that he chose to take her to his formal function, yet left his wife home. The nerve!

"Mom, I know you think Daddy is trying to be with other girls, but he said he really is not. He even cried and said you never believe him. He's your husband. You have to trust him, just like Grandma says. I'm going to trust my husband, especially if he's like Daddy. He always does nice things for you, but you never appreciate anything."

Wow! My fifteen-year-old, naïve child was trying to counsel me. And my dear mother—I didn't know what I was going to do about her.

"Okay, Julie. I won't divorce your dad," I said to appease her. I was annoyed by the conversation.

She was so excited. She even hugged me. "Thank you Mommy! I would be so embarrassed if you did. Maybe you and Dad should take a vacation together somewhere—just the two of you. It might help if you let Daddy do fun things with you sometimes."

I gave her a fake smile. "Sounds like a good plan. I'll speak with your father about it."

"Yay! You rock!" She hugged me again before running up to her room.

I waited up for Derrick so I could let him have it. He came home right as we were about to leave for church. He said he was in his office working all night and accidentally dozed off. He told us to go on without him, again, and he'd get some rest while we were gone. He promised the kids dinner out at an all-you-can-eat buffet when we returned. That made everything all right in their eyes.

Julie had to remind me while we were out, "See, I told you Daddy was trying to do fun stuff."

Little did she know, this wasn't the fun stuff her father had in mind.

Chapter 25

After extensive thought and soul searching, I sent Derrick a text message saying, "Okay, I'll do it." That was at eleven o'clock in the morning. He never replied, but ironically, he was home in time for dinner with the family, and he was ready for bed by ten. He wasn't sick. Without discussion, he knew what I meant. When I walked into the bedroom and saw the smut plastered across the television screen, along with the "gift box" sitting up on the dresser, I immediately became nauseous. But I told him I would, so there was no turning back now.

I did everything to fight my tears. I don't think I had ever felt so humiliated or degraded in my life. The things he did to me and had me doing to myself. After a while, I couldn't hold back the tears.

"Oh my goodness, Janelle! Why must you mess up every good thing? We were having a great time. I'm sure you were enjoying yourself. What are you crying for? You really get on my nerves."

"You might be used to this with your other women, but this—all of this—is degrading."

"Other women? Here you go with the stupid talk again. You keep letting your imagination run away from you. I keep telling you those pills have made you nutty. Don't forget, it was you who sent me a message saying you wanted this. Now are we going to do this, or am I going to another room tonight? I'm not going to stay in here with you and your madness. You're so worried about me being with another woman, but you need to be asking yourself what you are doing to make sure that doesn't happen. You're always pushing me away with something and then have the nerve to be insecure." He laughed. "You can't have it both ways. So tell me, what will it be?"

I sat for a minute while he looked at me, seriously waiting for an answer. I thought back to my conversation with Mother Hill. "Okay."

"Okay, okay?" he asked, with a grin I hated.

"Yes."

"Well are you going to stop with the stupid crying nonsense? I can't deal with that. It's a mood killer."

"Fine. Give me a moment to get myself together." I got up to go to the bathroom, where I cried some more while I ran the water.

When I returned, he happily did his thing and strongly suggested that I try to act like I was enjoying myself. He wanted to see me smiling.

Despite feeling raped by my own husband, I tried my best to act to his expectation. But when the ordeal was all said and done, and I heard him say, "Next time . . ." I broke down again. The thought of having to ever endure such abuse again was more than my mind could stand for that moment.

While I laid there trying to hide my crying, out of nowhere, Derrick announced, "By the way, I have to leave for another business trip tomorrow. I'm not sure how long I'll be gone. I'll let you know. Hopefully, while I'm gone, you'll learn to appreciate me for even trying to keep some spice in our marriage."

"Huh?" I sat up angry and confused. I hadn't heard of any business trip before that moment. After I allowed him to humiliate me, he was going to punish me with a fictitious business trip!

"I thought I told you about it."

"No, no you didn't. Is this another one of your punishments?"

"You're not a child. How do you feel I punish you? If anything, you're always punishing me with your never-ending insecurity."

"Once upon a time you'd take me on business trips with you. Since this new position, you stay out late, you stay out all night, you're always going away from your family, yet you call me insecure."

"Janelle, that was before, when we didn't have to worry about the children, and I had a job with much less responsibility than I have now."

"And how come you've never invited me to see your new office? Do you know how embarrassing it is for me to say I've never seen my husband's office? I don't even know any of your colleagues anymore, but yet you wonder why I might be insecure."

"Your insecurity is why you've never met any of them. I automatically know that you'd look at some of the women and swear I have something going on with them. Then you'd probably cause a scene like you did in church a while back with Sister Carmen. You're insecure in church. No! Nope! You won't see my office until you grow up."

"Fine! I don't want to see your stupid office," I childishly rebutted.

At least he laughed this time instead of storming out of the bedroom like always. "Goodnight, Janelle, and thank you for indulging me," he said before turning off the light.

I'll admit it did feel good for him to hold me.

Chapter 26

They could call me insecure all they'd like, but what I wouldn't be was anybody's fool.

I picked up the mail as usual and found a statement from a credit card company in the stack of mail. I had never seen a statement nor any mail from this company before. It was addressed to Derrick. There was a P.O. Box number written underneath our street address. Underneath that box was "Memphis, TN" plus our zip code in Collierville. Obviously, someone had made a boo-boo.

I typically didn't open any mail addressed to Derrick, which is rare in itself, aside from the normal household bills. However, as his wife, I felt I had every right to open any mail that financially impacted us both.

As suspected, it was a credit card statement with a ten-thousand-dollar credit line. There wasn't much activity on it, but I could tell it wasn't his first statement. There was a note on the bill that said, "Thank you for your payment of $2,678.93." I would have loved to see that statement. What could he have possibly bought for that amount, and how was he able to pay it off in one payment without pulling it from our bank account? I felt like I didn't even know my husband anymore. This bill was for $941.26. There were six local hotel charges, a $200 grocery charge, and an $80 Victoria Secret charge.

I had to take a seat. It was getting hard for me to breathe as I imagined him dancing around one of his bimbos, modeling lingerie in a hotel. Yet, I was insecure for no reason? Derrick seemed to have an explanation for everything. I could just hear him saying the hotel charges were from nights when I was just so incorrigible that he couldn't come home, and I could hear him say how he bought $200 worth of groceries for a needy family. But what could he say about Victoria Secret? That he bought underwear for a homeless woman on the street to have something fresh to change into? That'd be the story he tried to tell, but it certainly wasn't a story I'd be buying. And what about last month's charges? He spent close to $3000.

I decided to rifle though Derrick's papers in his office. I wasn't sure what I expected to find in there, but I was annoyed to find everything safely locked away. How convenient! I attempted to pick the locks, but that was an epic fail. The harder I tried and failed, the angrier I became. I went up to his closet to search every pocket, every drawer, and every hat box. Still nothing.

My women's intuition took me to the basement to search the other guest bedroom he hung out in, next to the game room. To my dismay, I found a condom wrapper and a stretched-out condom behind the bed. I couldn't tell if the condom was used, but it had most certainly been there for a while. The room had been cleaned a couple of times, but I guess I never thought to look behind the bed. I sat down, overwhelmed by my imagination as I cried.

Then rage started setting in. I had a sudden desire to go back to the gun range. I hadn't been back since my run-in with Willard Barker. I was hoping I wouldn't run into him again, because I'd be tempted to shoot him if he bothered me.

As luck would have it, he was there giving lessons to some youthful beauty. *Hmm, maybe he does give professional lessons to make money on the side.* With twins, I couldn't knock his hustle. I could only imagine how many other kids he had. Most were probably grown.

So while I was busy doing my own thing, I heard someone talking right behind me. I turned around to see Willard.

"Did you say something to me?" I asked, moving one of my ear covers and trying to get away from his exceeding closeness.

"I said, I see you're 'hubby' practicing again. There's a whole lot of rage there."

"Beat it! Get lost. Go mind your own business!" I yelled. I almost cried as I fought the urge to turn the gun on him. I couldn't believe how upset I was, and maybe he was right. I imagined Derrick was the target and annihilated his groin area and his head.

"I'm really just trying to be your friend. I know we got off to a bad start, but I actually admire you. You got spunk," he said, looking me over like a woman on her cycle looks at Godiva chocolates. I felt violated by his eyes.

"I don't want to be your friend, and if you don't get away from me, I'm going to shoot you too."

"Too? As in also?" He started walking away with a smile, shaking his head.

I suddenly regretted my words. I was pretty certain they'd come back to haunt me some day.

Chapter 27

After I learned that Kenny was gay, it seemed easier to talk to him and just be myself. It was almost like having a best girlfriend, except he was a guy. He was very masculine, and still very handsome. Kenny and I would find humor in discussing accounting or business. When I was with him, or even speaking to him on the phone, I was happy. He understood me, my work, my schedule—he just got me. Derrick didn't want to know anything about my work or clients, other than that I had some.

Kenny had an eye for fashion. Rather than tell me I looked tacky, he'd say, "Girl, you know what would look good on you?" and then I'd get it for myself. On a couple of occasions, Kenny would pick up a couple of items for me, and gift me with them. He said he loved women's fashions and enjoyed shopping for the various women in his life, to include me. I didn't dare tell Derrick that some gorgeous man was buying me nice gifts, even if the man was gay and unavailable.

On this particular day, instead of the full lunch experience, Kenny and I opted for gelato and scones while we talked shop.

"I know we haven't known each other that long, but you seem different today. I can't put my finger on it. And no disrespect, but you have bags underneath your eyes. I know you've been laughing at all of my corny jokes, but what's going on?"

I appreciated the mere fact that he bothered to inquire. I could hear my momma screaming in my head about letting people inside my marriage, but after that last dinner, her words don't hold much weight.

I dug into my pocketbook and pulled out the credit card statement I had been carrying around. I handed it to Kenny and his brow furrowed as he took it all in.

"Did you confront him about this?"

"No, not yet. He's away on another one of his business trips. I believe he said Destin, Florida this time. Actually, I've been thinking about how I want to approach this revelation. Could it be innocent?"

I dug into my pocketbook again as Kenny surveyed the statement.

"I don't know. It doesn't seem innocent. Did you know about this credit card?" he asked just as his eyes widened at the previous statement balance. "Whoa! Wait! What the heck is this? Twenty-six hundred last month? Did he dip in your bank accounts to pay it?"

"No and, no, I didn't know the card existed. I don't know how long he's had it and I don't know that post office box, but I decided to do some snooping around for other evidence of foul play, and I found this." I discreetly showed him the small baggie I'd placed the condom and wrapper in.

Kenny covered his mouth and then asked, "Where'd you find this at?"

"Would you believe in my own home? I went to check one of our guest bedrooms he likes to hang out in—to punish me. I don't know what made me look behind the bed. That's where I found it. I'm not sure how long it's been there, but I'm sure he'll find a way to explain it away like everything else."

"Does anyone else sleep in that room?" Kenny asked.

"Only Derrick. It's supposed to be for if we have a lot of company. We have a game room down there next to that bedroom, so sometimes he hangs out there after playing with the boys, and he'll do whatever it is he does down there. He calls it, 'The Man Cave.' I was so upset that I actually went to the gun range to assassinate an imaginary Derrick. I was certain to leave no groin area untouched."

Kenny laughed, causing me to laugh.

"Uh-oh! Sounds like someone had better get their act together. Quick!" Kenny said.

"Tell me about it. I couldn't believe I was actually there thinking about killing my husband."

Kenny laughed again. I was glad my feelings of rage were dissipating. This is why I enjoyed the friend I found in Kenny.

"Okay, Big Sis—I'm going to call you my big sister from here on—but anyhow, what you need to do is take charge of your marriage. Tell your husband that you are planning a romantic getaway for the two of you, and if he doesn't go with you, you'll go alone. That's all you need. There's too much distrust, and you have every reason to feel the way you do. I'd be ready to beat the brakes off of somebody if I found out my husband had a secret credit card and was spending thousands of dollars on it, paid for with a bank account I knew nothing of."

"Exactly! And that's what had me at the range." I rolled my eyes. Kenny had me on the edge of my seat with talk of taking charge of my marriage. However, I sat back on my seat at the thought of my husband secretly spending our money on only God knows what, reminding me that I want to kill him.

"Uh, no. I didn't say I'd do all of that now, but I'm just saying you have every reason to be upset. Not to go Rambo or anything, but upset." Kenny paused for a moment of thought and looked around at the people passing before he continued. "Honestly, if you saw your husband butt naked with another woman in your home, or in your bed, there would be a high probability that you'd still stay with him after that. He'd be remorseful and even act right for a while, but then he'd probably go back to his doggish ways. Most women stay in those relationships. I don't know why, but they do. My point is, despite what you've found and now know, you're still going to stick with him, so why say anything? Just do what you must to block every opportunity for him to cheat."

"Wow! You're sounding like Mother Hill." I laughed.

"Who's that?"

"She's the first lady at my church—the pastor's wife. She imparted similar words of wisdom to me on more than one occasion. She's been with her husband almost sixty years. I'm sure she has plenty of stories of situations she's had to endure."

"Wow! Sixty years? That's a long time. So now you know what I say to you must be correct. You're going to have to keep your fashion game on fleek—always! Not just once in a while. I remember that day you came out with that pencil skirt and those Christian Louboutin shoes. I was checking you out, and I'm gay. You were looking GOOD! That's what your husband wants and needs to see all the time. He'll start paying you more attention."

I recalled that day when I arrived home and Derrick was quite pleased. I hadn't dressed like that since, despite all of Kenny's fashion advice and the many new items purchased. I smiled from the memory. Finding out Kenny was gay might have had something to do with my lack of dressing to impress.

"See, you know I'm right. I bet your husband snatched you up good that day, didn't he?"

We both laughed.

"You're right. I have to admit it. He even told me I was sexy. That meant so much to me. We were in a good place for a while after that."

"Don't think just because I'm gay that I don't understand what a man looks for in a woman. Hell, I expect my husband to look sexy and desirable, and I try to do the same. You have to stroke that man's ego and remind him that you are a beautiful woman who's attracted to him. I bet all those young, perky college girls remind him on a daily basis."

The thought of it made me cringe—Derrick in his office with the large desk and sofa Julie told me about, along with those college girls stroking his ego for a grade change.

Kenny continued. "And you need to stop letting your imagination run away from you. I can see by the change in your demeanor that you're thinking about him with those young girls. The reality is, he may be, but if you want your husband to be with you and not with them, then you're going to have to step up your game. Go on a shopping spree for yourself and replace any frumpy, old-lady clothes in your closet. Don't even keep them for church. Work that make-up. Then you plan a getaway, and watch him be right there with you and all over you. You're too beautiful for him to be looking elsewhere. Stop giving him reason to."

"But what about the fact that he's always gone and he won't even see my outfits or me?" I asked my friendly advisor, frustrated by my situation.

"Love, trust me when I tell you, word will eventually get back to him and he'll hang around a bit more to see for himself."

I suddenly thought about my big-mouth kids, and then smiled. "You might be onto something."

"And whatever you do, don't take him to South Beach in Miami. That's a recipe for disaster. Take him to San Francisco or San Diego. Take in a breathtaking sunset. Dress up and head to the theater. Dine at the fine restaurants, where you get to look your best. And make sure you take your own trip to Victoria's Secret. Get him in the habit of buying lingerie for you to wear. Up your shoe game in the bedroom. Don't do the furry slippers. Lingerie must be worn with heels."

"In the bedroom?" I asked, perplexed by the thought.

"Especially in the bedroom. You better buy shoes tailor-made for a sexy night in the bedroom. What'll happen is, when your husband sees you fully clothed in business attire, he'll see you with some sexy shoes on and he'll wanna rock your world. He'll be thinking about the nights when you have those sexy shoes on with the lingerie, for his eyes only."

"Okay, I'm going to try it, but if it doesn't work, I'm going to think about you when I go to the gun range the next time." I laughed.

"It'll work. Trust me, next time we talk, you'll be complaining about getting too much attention. He'll be stalking you instead of trying to stay away from you. And don't forget, if he doesn't agree to the vacation, tell him you'll just go alone. That'll drive him crazy—especially if you pack the sexy underwear and shoes."

I was feeling giddy. Kenny had me all pumped up. He'd make an excellent life coach. Now all I had to do was build up my confidence enough to execute the game plan.

After our dessert lunch, we skipped over to this small shoe boutique Kenny frequented to purchase a collection of shoes for me. I paid for four pairs, and he paid for another three. He wanted me to shop there for shoes from that point on instead of department stores, where I typically went. I knew one thing— those shoes were so sexy that I was getting turned on by the thought of a night with them on. Kenny also advised me to never reveal my whole collection all at once. That way Derrick would always be lurking to see what I had next.

Chapter 28

f I wasn't living it, I wouldn't have believed it was my life. Everything Kenny said to me was perfect. I lost track of how many compliments I received from Derrick. He was coming home in time for dinner to see what I was wearing, and every night was the Fourth of July in the bedroom. There was no working late, no hanging out with the boys, and no mysterious business trips. He was a bit opposed to the idea of a trip to San Francisco, but when I let him know I already planned it, with my itinerary, he suddenly found the time.

Unfortunately, I had to get Brittany to babysit for part of our vacation. I couldn't find anyone else who could stay for a few days. Mom agreed to come babysit for the first part of our five-night, romantic adventure, but she couldn't stay the whole time. Janae volunteered, but Derrick was adamant that she would never babysit his children ever again. So that left Brittany. I figured it wasn't such a big deal since she wouldn't be around my husband.

The first part of our time spent in San Francisco was wonderful, peaceful, and romantic. We had so much fun and made so much love in our suite, which offered a perfect view of the sunset. We took in a play, did some shopping together, and he even picked out some lingerie and shoes he wanted to see me in. But all of that turned with the tide—or should I say, with the changing of babysitters.

I swear that girl was calling Derrick's phone like every hour on the hour. She would complain about Julie being disrespectful and not listening. Then she'd call to ask if it was okay to eat something ridiculous that there was no reason to ask. I don't know why I didn't realize that Brittany had a childlike mentality, despite her womanly physique.

Derrick was getting so irritated by the situation that he started snapping at me. He accused me of not properly planning the trip, so Brittany didn't have to babysit. Her last call to Derrick was when she called to say the baby was moving around a lot. He yelled at her and told her not to call his phone again.

That evening we were scheduled to have a romantic dinner in Jack London's Square and then planned to catch a jazz show nearby. However, while I was trying to get Derrick back in a romantic frame of mind, my phone kept ringing over and over. We tried to ignore it, but it was persistent. We looked and saw the calls were coming from home. Needless to say, we both began to panic. I called home and Julie answered the phone.

"What's going on?" I asked.

"Nothing," she casually answered.

"Well, who keeps calling my phone like that? They called five times."

"Your silly babysitter. She said her stomach was hurting and she didn't know if something was wrong with her baby. I think her feelings were hurt because Daddy yelled at her and told her to stop calling his phone. So she called your phone instead." Julie laughed.

I had the phone on speaker and then Derrick told Julie to put Brittany on. Brittany came to the phone crying.

"Brittany, what is going on with you? Why'd you say you'd babysit if you knew you had a problem with it?" Derrick snapped.

"I didn't know I'd have a problem. Julie's been so mean and hurtful since I've arrived. Once Janelle's mother left, she's been even worse, and making the boys be disobedient. She told them they didn't have to listen to me, because I am a retard."

"She said what?" Derrick yelled.

"She said I was a retard and I don't even know who the father of my baby is, so the boys have been laughing at me and making fun of me. I think the stress is upsetting the baby and now I don't feel well," Brittany said before sobbing into the phone.

"Brittany, put Julie back on the phone, please. We'll talk to her and the boys," I said, hoping to salvage our vacation.

But that was too much like right . . .

"No, Brittany, don't put them on the phone. We'll be on the next flight home and do not let them know we are coming. Do you think you can hold on until then?" Derrick asked.

Brittany's smile was so bright I could see the rays through the phone. She suddenly sounded so happy.

And me, I was so upset.

"But Derrick, do we really have to leave now?" I asked after he ended the call. "We could have talked to the kids over the phone. They certainly would have listened to you."

"I knew this was a bad idea from the start. I let you force me to do something I was opposed to doing in the first place. We had no business going this far away from the kids without proper supervision for days."

I agreed with the latter statement. "I should have planned better for a babysitter. I was just so anxious to keep the fire going between us. I didn't want to lose it. I knew this trip would help us get to a better place, and everything was going great until now. Could you at least give me credit for trying?" My eyes pleaded with his as he gave me an icy glare.

Rather than answer, he said, "Hurry, let's get packing so we can get to the airport."

I wanted to cry, but I didn't dare. I knew he'd yell at me and call me names. Instead, I sucked it up and did as told. I was so looking forward to the seafood dinner at Scotts and Brian Culbertson's jazz piano at Yoshi's. *Maybe next time.*

When we were seated on the plane back to Memphis, I was shocked Derrick that reached over and kissed me unexpectedly. "Thank you, baby, for trying. I really did appreciate everything you planned for us, and I had a great time with my beautiful wife."

I don't know if the plane had taken off yet, but I was definitely on a cloud.

Although we made it home at close to two in the morning, Derrick was so annoyed with Brittany that he woke her from her peaceful sleep and drove her home in the middle of the night. He promptly returned home to try to salvage our romantic night, even though I was beyond exhausted.

I think Kenny may have been right when he said my next complaint would be getting too much time and attention. But I decided I'd bask in the glory for as long as I could.

Chapter 29

As I gathered Derrick's clothes together for the dry cleaners, I discovered a thick stack of papers folded in an envelope and tucked in his jacket pocket. I'm not sure how he would miss such important looking papers sticking up out of the pocket. I opened the envelope and unfolded the blue pages. They were insurance papers. There was a one-million-dollar policy with my name and one with each of the children's names. On each policy, Derrick was listed as the only beneficiary.

I held the papers in my hand and went and took a seat on the lounge chair in the bedroom. I was trying not to let my imagination run away from me, but a sudden, chilling fear crept inside of me.

Not sure who else I could call, I called Kenny.

"Hey, Big Sis! What's up?" he answered all cheery.

"Kenny, I think my husband might be planning to kill me and the children. I just found a policy for each of us with Derrick listed as the sole beneficiary." I was getting angrier as I spoke. I really wanted to give Derrick a piece of my mind, but I decided to let Kenny talk me off the ledge.

"Wow! I don't know what to say about that. Was there not any discussion first? How big is the policy? I assume it must be huge to scare you like this."

"It's for one million dollars each, which means, if we all die, he'd get four million dollars. There have not been any discussions about these policies. We already bought policies long ago, and they're only a fraction of that amount.

Now I feel like I have to keep watch on how he might kill us. He did just take my truck to get the service on it. Maybe that's how he'll do it."

Kenny laughed so hard, I was annoyed. You could hear him choking.

"It wasn't that funny, you know," I snapped.

"I'm sorry, love. You do crack me up sometimes. You have to stop thinking the worst in him. Everything's finally going great for you, and now you think he's trying to kill you. Stop it!"

"I know he has at least two guns."

"And I have three, but I'm not trying to kill anyone. If he kills you, he'll be in jail and get nothing. Your husband doesn't even know you go to the gun range and pretend that he's the target. I know you're not trying to kill him no matter what gibberish you speak, but if he knew, don't you think he'd be alarmed just because you've been hiding the fact that you practice? Of course *we* know you are not a threat to your husband's life, but he might feel reasonably threatened. I say that to say, although your intentions aren't harmful, sometimes they can be perceived that way by others."

"So you think I have no reason for concern?"

"Where did you find the papers? In a safe?"

"No, it was in his jacket pocket. I was gathering his clothes for the cleaners and it was in his suit jacket."

"Well, I'm sure he wasn't hiding them from you. Maybe he intended to discuss them with you, but got side-tracked by your sexiness," Kenny said with a chuckle. "I can hear you over there smiling," he teased.

I was. Kenny made me feel better, again.

"What would my life be without you in it?" I confessed.

"They'd be locking you up in a nuthouse right about now."

We laughed.

"Probably. Thank you, Lil Bro."

"Lil Bro?"

"Well, I can't be your big sis if you're not my lil bro."

"Yeah, I guess that makes sense. Anywho, I got work to do and money to be made, and so do you. Stop snooping!"

"Thanks again for putting up with me," I said before hanging up.

I left the papers on the dresser for Derrick to see. I wanted to see if he would try to hide them from me or discuss it with me.

"Oh good, you found them," he said when he got in and saw the papers. "I left them in my jacket for you to find. I didn't want to leave it on the dresser, in case the kids came into the room. I wanted you to look it over and tell me if you think it's sufficient. I have another one on myself for five million. I think that should take care of you and the kids."

I felt *sooooo* stupid. When will I learn?

"That's a lot," I said.

"With today's economy, it's not enough. The policies we have wouldn't get you a decent home anywhere. The costs for burials start around $10,000. I'd rather you had a lot than too little. If you're okay with it, I'll need you to sign the form to be co-beneficiary for the children's policy. God forbid something was to happen to me and one of the kids."

I was so in love with my husband. I couldn't believe how thoughtful he was becoming. I felt so guilty for thinking the worst, as usual.

The following day I called and updated Kenny. I let him know he was right, as always.

Chapter 30

was half tempted to skip Bible Study tonight. This would be the third straight one Derrick missed. At least for the first two, he had the decency to let me know ahead of time. But this time, he actually told me he'd meet me there, and now it was 9:00pm and everyone was heading to their respective homes, rejuvenated by the holy word, while my joy was siphoned from me as I foolishly sat in wait for my no-show husband.

I was hoping to quietly slip out of the door before I had to answer any more questions regarding Derrick's absence. I certainly didn't want to tell anyone that I had no clue where my husband was at, nor did he have the courtesy to send me a text message saying he wasn't going to make it.

"Sister Roberts," Minister Hill called out, before I could make my escape to the children's church to collect my children.

"Minister Hill, how are you? I loved your message this evening."

He came and gave me a hug, which was something he had never done before. After all the tales I'd heard about him, I felt violated. It was an odd feeling, because I'd been hugged by ministers back in Nashville, and it always seemed innocent. Maybe it seemed odd because Minister Hill hadn't ever attempted to hug me when Derrick was present.

"Thank you so much for your kind words. Too bad so many were absent tonight and missed the message. Even my own niece has been skipping my Bible Study lately, always blaming everything on that pregnancy of hers. All of my nieces, and she's the only person afflicted by a pregnancy. And speaking of absent, I've noticed Brother Derrick has been missing lately. Momma—I mean First Lady—told me you've been having some problems on the home front and thought maybe you could use some prayer to help you get through your storm."

"Storm?" I asked, both confused and annoyed. I felt like First Lady Hill betrayed my confidence by discussing my private matters with her son. Who cares if he was supposed to be a minister? He was a minister as a result of a family business, and certainly not by some calling from on high. He was the epitome of a sinner, or so I've heard, and he wanted me to see *him* for some prayer? Not in this lifetime.

"Well, maybe I'm just jumping to conclusions. This congregation keeps so many ugly rumors circulating and I thought maybe you were broken up by some of them."

My mouth fell open. I looked at Minister Hill as if he were crazy. How embarrassing, the thought of Derrick and I being the subject of church rumors. "Wow! I didn't know of any rumors. We're doing just fine. Derrick often takes business trips, which sometimes prevents him from attending church, but he is diligent about his family attending, even when he can't."

"Where is he tonight?" Minister Hill asked, almost cutting off my delusional rant.

"Huh?" I asked, feeling my stomach flip-flop, while trying to maintain a look of confidence regarding my husband's mysterious activities.

"Where is your husband tonight? I couldn't help but take notice of how you spent the evening as if you were looking for him to come through the door any moment . . . but he didn't. I'm sure you also noticed Sister Carmen also didn't show up tonight. You know, she's never missed a Bible Study? Not even when she had the flu. It just kind of goes hand-in-hand with some of the rumors floating around."

I most certainly did take notice that both Carmen and Brittany were missing, while my husband led me to believe that he'd be here tonight. I desperately wanted to cry, just as much as I wanted to tell Minister Hill that he was evil. Pure evil. Why would he want to plant such ugly seeds in my mind?

He quickly answered. "Sister Roberts, I think you should come by my office tomorrow for prayer. I know you have a very busy schedule, so if you'd prefer, you could meet me at my home office and I could have some lunch prepared for you, since you'll probably be pressed for time."

"Do you think my husband will be okay if I told him I was going to your house to discuss his infidelities over lunch? I'd think he'd be downright angry and would decide that we could no longer attend this church anymore."

"Sis-Sister Roberts," he stuttered with nervous anger, "are you trying to imply that I am offering anything ungodly by suggesting the preparation of lunch to accommodate your busy schedule? Also, I am not saying that your husband is being unfaithful, but I know you are already plagued with insecurities, which is why I offered to help you in prayer—to conquer those demons before they take over your marriage."

He made it sound so innocent and me so foolish. I was embarrassed.

"I'm sorry. I don't know what came over me. Things have been a bit crazy lately, and I've been on edge."

He hugged me again. "All is forgiven, Sister. I just want you to be well. Mother is also concerned about you, which is why she came to me and asked if I could help. She really loves you. She never takes this much interest in any of the other women. I typically like to speak with both parties at the same time, but based on Mother's conversation, I wasn't too sure if your husband was aware that you were seeking guidance for your marriage. I'd really love to help you both, but I just need to get to the root of the issue, and I'm sure you won't be quite as open in your husband's presence.

He was right. I could never spill my guts about Derrick in front of Derrick. I couldn't help but visualize him choking me again if he knew.

"Minister Hill, I really appreciate your offer of support, but I don't want to anger or disrespect my husband. He would be quite upset if he knew I was having meetings about him."

"This is why I want to pray with you through this storm. You shouldn't have to weather this storm on your own. Lean not unto your own understanding, Sister."

He was almost sounding desperate. I'd heard so many rumors about the entire Hill family that I didn't know what to believe.

It was like he was reading my mind when he said, "Sister Roberts, I know you've heard so many nasty rumors about my family going around this church that you don't know who you can trust, but I want you to know, they are rumors. Just like the rumors about your husband being with Sister Carmen. I've already spoken with her on the matter and she says there is nothing between them. And tonight, I'm sure there'll be new rumors with them both missing. This is why I want to help you. This is why I want you to be prayed up and able to weather the storm."

I smiled. "Okay, I'll set up an appointment, but I can't make it this week. My schedule is way too full. I'd have to work it in."

"Well, don't take too long. You know that the Devil will keep you busy to keep your marriage in jeopardy."

"Yeah, you're right. Definitely next week. I promise." I smiled and he hugged me yet again.

My phone vibrated, letting me know that I had a text message. I looked at my phone. "Oh, that's Derrick now, letting me know he's outside with the kids. But thank you, and I'll make that appointment for sure."

Minister Hill seemed a little disappointed with the news of Derrick being outside, but he still managed to say, "Great!" before moving along about his business.

Before I could make it out of the door, I was met by Jocelyn.

"Your hubby is waiting outside, but I want you to know he was with Carmen before he got here. She sent me a text saying, as always, it was all that and then some, and she can't wait for more." Jocelyn showed me the text on her large iPhone screen. "I called her while you were talking to Minister Hill, and she said it's just a matter of time before he is all hers. She doesn't want to keep sharing him, not even with me. I have to admit, he's great. I can't get enough, personally. I can't imagine giving him up."

"You are such a liar." I laughed. "Trust me, he doesn't want any of you. I also know where my husband was this evening," I lied, trying to sound confident.

"You think you know. Oh, and I guarantee you, he brought home some banana pudding cake for you tonight. You like banana pudding, right? Well, Carmen sent him home with some cake for you and the kids. Enjoy it!" She wickedly laughed and walked off toward a different exit.

I had to take a seat to regroup before I went out to face Derrick and the kids. I walked outside to find each of them eating banana pudding cake like they didn't have a care in the world. He greeted me like a loving husband who was missing his wife. I started to give him grief about his absence and the cake, but I decided not to, chalking the whole thing up to another of Jocelyn's antics of trying to get under my skin.

However, as loving as he was, he sent me off to bed alone so he could do some work for most of the night. I cried myself to sleep again.

Chapter 31

Meeting with Minister Hill would probably rank at the top of the list of the stupidest things I'd ever done. I knew Minister Hill was evil, so I don't know why I agreed to meet him privately. Probably had something to do with Derrick having the nerve to feed my children the spoils of his mistress. Somehow, Minister Hill convinced me to change out of my pantsuit into a Japanese kimono for our Japanese lunch, which actually was delicious.

Long story short, he kissed me without resistance and touched my naked body. Well actually, he kissed and touched my naked body without resistance. I don't know how it happened. It was Kenny's ten calls that stopped things from going any further.

As much as I'd like to say he must have drugged me from the first glass of wine, because I had no legitimate explanation of why I would change out of my clothes, I believe my wrath toward Derrick played a role. All of Minister Hill's talk of removing the kimono to liberate my soul seems really ridiculous in hindsight. The oils that he rubbed my body with were supposed to be a protection from the evils that were trying to overcome me. There was no explanation for the kissing, other than the oil rubbing made me horny.

I can't believe as ugly and despicable as Minister Hill was, I wanted every bit of what he was offering. That's why I was rejecting all of Kenny's persistent calls. Minister Hill made me feel desirable and appreciated, while he filled my head with stories of how my husband was getting it on with half the women in the church and his school. He spoke in great detail, as if he was in the room watching them.

The more Minister Hill talked, licked, and touched me, the more I wanted him inside of me. The more I thought about my husband feeding my children cake from that Jezebel, the more I wanted to hurt him. I thought about shooting Derrick, but as lust overtook me, I felt it would be the perfect revenge, and I'd have my neglected needs satisfied at the same time.

When I finally took Kenny's call, it was about a half billion-dollar client he was trying to give to me. That brought everything to a halt. For the moment, I had no regrets about my actions with Minister Hill. However, as the effects of the wine I had no business drinking wore off completely, I was horrified by my actions as I replayed each disgusting scene in my mind, over and over again. I even threw up a couple of times. Worse, I couldn't tell a soul. Well, I didn't tell Kenny at first, but I told him a few days later when I met with him and he realized something was very wrong.

Kenny scolded me. You would have thought he was my husband the way he carried on. He was very disappointed and more disappointed to know it was his calls that stopped me from going all the way.

Ironically, Derrick hadn't seemed to notice or so I thought. He hadn't said anything to make me think he'd noticed. The more he avoided the bedroom, the more I'd wonder if he knew about Minister Hill.

That Sunday in church was especially difficult for me. My emotions were all over the place. Not only did Jocelyn and Carmen seem to spend the entire service flirting with Derrick, but I was lusting over Minister Hill. I felt his eyes undressing me as he sat in the pulpit.

By the following Tuesday, I couldn't stand it any longer. I went back for "prayer" after Derrick left for another of his so-called business trips, neglecting my needs. I was so totally fed up with Derrick's treatment.

Kenny would have been my first choice for stepping outside of my marriage, but unfortunately, he was not an option on the table. Minister Hill was. A desperate option, but one I knew I'd never have to worry about getting back to Derrick.

Minister Hill sent me home totally satisfied, and the scariest thing about it all was that I didn't have a single regret. I finally felt vindicated for all the neglect and hell I'd endured from Derrick. That is, until I arrived home that evening and Derrick was home. He had a romantic night all planned out for me, with rose petals, candles, champagne, chocolate strawberries—the works. His apology for neglecting me for work cut me to the core.

Then came, "Baby, I think we should find a new church. I just don't like all the craziness going on in our church. I don't know how many times I've heard that I was having an affair with the women in there, and I know they aren't too respectful to you. I don't like that. You should be able to have friends in the church as you did back home. It makes no sense that your only friend is an old lady who is the Pastor's wife, or their teenaged granddaughter. I think since we've been here, I've been really selfish and not putting you as the priority. Julie reminded me yesterday that you have never even been to my new office, which is crazy. Tomorrow, I want you to come to my office and we'll have lunch together. I want everyone to meet my sexy wife that I've been hiding for some reason or another."

I was too stunned for words.

He continued while we relaxed in the bath together, surrounded by rose petals and candles. "I have to start showing you how important you are to me. I know it seems like I take you for granted, but I do notice everything you do for me, the kids, and our entire family. And I have no business letting other people disrespect you the way those women at church do. It's no wonder you are insecure. I think I'd lose my mind if some other man tried to be with my wife. I'd be ready to kill you both."

I cringed. I was praying the bath water would soothe the vaginal swelling I was experiencing from the good beating Minister Hill had put on me less than twelve hours earlier. The guilt was eating me alive. I was actually planning on seeing Minister Hill the following day for yet another round, because I just knew Derrick was off on one of his rendezvous that he calls business trips. Everything in me wanted to know why he was home instead of away like he said he would be.

Later that night, after the romance, I fell asleep. Derrick woke me up with rage in his eyes. He was fully dressed and holding my phone. I couldn't imagine what had him so upset.

"Janelle, how could you?" he asked.

"How could I what?" I was confused. I couldn't think of anything incriminating in my phone. Then I thought about some of my communications with Kenny via text, but couldn't recall anything damning.

"So, you've been lying to me all of this time about Kenny, huh? I see he called you one day about ten times. You talk or meet almost daily. You tell me he's some gay, married man helping you with your business, yet you have pictures of his penis in your phone, from today. I know something didn't feel right, which is why I looked in your phone. And now I see my wife is a common whore."

"Derrick, I swear to you—"

"Shut up!" he yelled before smacking me. "You are a lying slut."

I was about to protest again, but then I noticed the gun sitting on the nightstand. I became terrified. I wanted to clear Kenny's name at the very least. I really had no idea what picture he was speaking of. I could only think of Minister Hill, since he said it was from that day. I vaguely remembered him saying he was going to give me something to think about to get me through my days, but I just assumed that was the sex itself.

"I have been sitting here for almost an hour, thinking about what to do to you, but then I realized that anything I could do to you would hurt my children. However, I think now would be a good time to be honest with you. I'm sure it will hurt you, because by now you must know I will never touch you again."

"Derrick, I have never been with Kenny. I've been wanting you to meet him. If you met him, you'd know."

Derrick picked up the gun and pushed it to my mouth. "Didn't I tell you to shut up? I dare you to say another word. No matter how you slice this, you're a lying, cheating whore. I bet half those times you told me you were bleeding, you knew you were with some other man and was worried about me finding out, as I did tonight."

"Derrick—" I said before he punched me in my face with the hand that previously held my phone.

"I'm not even going to be mad at you. I'll never touch you again, but I'm not going to be mad at you. I slept with Brittany right here in this bed," he patted the bed with a huge smile. "And it was good. Really good. As a matter of fact, we've been together while you were in here sleeping. I've been with Kathy too, but she wasn't as freaky as Brittany, nor was her butt as big, so she had to go. You already know I've been with Jocelyn and Carmen. Sometimes together. But what you didn't know was I also had Carmen here in this bed while you guys went to Brentwood for those family dinners without me. When I go on business trips, I never go alone. I usually have some hot, young girl to keep me warm at night. Oh, and by the way, I am in love with Carmen and Brittany, but I was willing to break things off with all of them for the sake of our marriage. Besides, I know they sleep around way too much for me to settle down with them.

"But now, as for you and I, we will stay married for our children, but know I won't ever touch you again. I have way too many options for that. And you'd be surprised what most of these young girls would do for a grade change, which is why I never invited you to my office. Stupid me, I was almost willing to give it all up for your whoring behind. Good thing I found out about you now.

"Remember that night when I skipped Bible Study to be with Carmen, and she gave me that delicious banana pudding cake for the kids? You know, that night you were setting up your prayer session with Minister Hill. Speaking of which, are you feeling cleansed now?" He laughed a deranged laugh.

How could he know?

He continued. "I did that because I was angry at you. I found a stretched condom in a sandwich bag. I was going to hurt you then, but then I found a credit card statement you were hiding that belongs to me. I take it that you were trying to gather evidence against me for something, but just know, you've been relieved of my property. I called Carmen just as she was about to make it to church and had her detour. As for those pictures Jocelyn showed you a while back, that was nothing compared to the photos I have of both of them on my phone—and every other girl I've been with. One last confession—about ninety percent of the time when I'm on the computer doing work throughout the night, it's not job related."

I wanted to scream and claw his eyes out while he smugly confessed his deeds, but he was still holding the gun.

"Get up and go stand in the corner! You need to be punished."

"What!" I asked in disbelief.

"You heard me. You deserve to be punished, don't you? And then I'm going to whip you with my belt."

"And what about you?" I boldly asked.

"What did you say to me?" he asked, pointing the gun at me again.

I cried as I slid off the bed to find a corner to stand. He laughed hysterically as he approached me with his belt.

"Janelle! Janelle! What's the matter with you?" Derrick yelled, turning on his nightstand light.

I was standing in the corner sobbing while he was lying under covers, awakened by my sobbing.

"Get back in this bed. Why are you standing in the corner naked and crying?" He got up and brought me back to the bed. He didn't have on the clothes I remembered him wearing while he had the gun. I looked around in the dimly lit room and didn't see any sign of a gun.

Oh my lord!! I'm losing my mind. I couldn't remember what was real and what wasn't real.

Did he confess his sexual conquests to me while pointing a gun at me?

Did he accuse me of having an affair? Did he know about my "prayer session" with Minister Hill?

He got a wet washcloth and cleaned up my face. He was so loving and kind. He repeatedly kissed me and reassured me that he was there and wasn't going anywhere. He told me he loved me and tucked me back into bed before cuddling up behind me, making me feel safe and protected from the Freddie Krueger that came to wreak havoc on my soul while I slept. Guilt is a horrible thing.

"Did you have a bad dream or something? That was pretty scary. I've never seen you sleepwalk, ever. I thought that was just television stuff."

I boo-hoo-hoo cried all over again. I couldn't believe none of it was real. I even wondered if my deed with Minister Hill was real, but that next day I saw the photo he put in my phone of his privates, and I knew that part was real. I quickly deleted it before my nightmare became a reality. I also deleted those back-to-back calls from Kenny.

When Derrick tried to get me to recall my dream, I told him I couldn't remember, but thought it might have had something to do with when I was a kid in school. Again, he told me I needed to see the doctor and get off of those pills, because sleepwalking was dangerous.

I reminded him that no pills would mean continual bleeding or surgery. He told me that I needed to find a way to get that surgery scheduled before someone got hurt.

So many times throughout the day, I wondered if I was really dreaming or was Derrick trying to make me think I was going crazy. However, when he *finally* had me come to his job and allowed me to meet his colleagues wearing the professional, sexy outfit he purchased for me, I knew there was no way that he figured out that I cheated on him with Minister Hill, and his hurtful confessions were just a figment of my imagination. I even found the condom and credit card statement hidden where I had placed them.

Nonetheless, the guilt was killing me and I didn't know what to do. I don't know what got into Derrick, but he was behaving as Husband of the Year.

I needed someone to talk to so, I told Kenny how I clearly recalled Derrick telling me about all of his affairs after accusing me of having one.

Kenny laughed at my foolishness and told me to take my secret to the grave. He also told me to stop sleepwalking before I started sleep-talking and accidentally named him as the person I was having an affair with.

Chapter 32

As per Derrick's advice, I went to see my doctor about the problems I was having with the hormone pills. She assured me my sleepwalking and nightmares were not in any way associated to the pills and suggested I seek mental health counseling. She ordered a bunch of tests to see what was going on with my fibrous condition. I was a bit alarmed when she called to have me to come in as soon as possible to discuss my results.

"Janelle, how have you been?" Dr. Suarez asked, beating around the bush.

"As well as to be expected, when one receives a 'drop everything and come now' call. You typically go over things by phone."

"I am sorry to cause you alarm. Hopefully by now you've made an appointment for a mental health evaluation?"

"Not as of yet. I have a few very important clients that someone has entrusted me with, along with my family. Not only that, my daughter's sweet sixteen is quickly approaching, and that has really been sucking up all of my time. I promise I will as soon as her party is over."

"Janelle, you need to see someone right away. Particularly after I go over your test results."

I could feel my air escaping me. *This must be really bad.*

"Am I dying?" I just asked, getting to the point.

She smiled, letting me know I was way off base. "Not anytime soon, from any of the tests I've done. Ironically, your fibroids are doing exceptionally well and might actually be gone on their own with a few more months of hormone therapy. Worst case scenario, a D&C might be in order, but you are no longer a candidate for a hysterectomy, as we originally discussed a few months ago."

"That's great news, isn't it?" I asked, confused and excited. I'm not sure how much more tolerable Derrick might be of my hormone pills, but at least I wouldn't have to be down for weeks after a surgery. I thought surely he'd be understanding since there was such great progress in my condition. He'd been so wonderful lately, I couldn't imagine him not being as excited.

Dr. Suarez had a somber look. "Well, yes, that's great news. However, that is not the reason I had you come in to see me today."

"Huh?" I felt a sucker punch coming.

"Based on the symptoms you complained of, I ran a tox screen, and it came back positive for small amounts of PCP and Ecstasy. That would explain your sleepwalking and hallucinations."

"Huh? What! I don't use drugs!"

"Well, at some point within the days before your blood work, you somehow ingested those items. That is definitely not something you want to be doing while taking those hormone pills, or at all," she seemingly scolded.

"But I swear . . ." I was ready to cry as I thought back to everything I had eaten or drunk those days leading up to my exam.

"Your other test shows you have Chlamydia."

"Oh, can't I just take antibiotics for that? That's what I had a couple of years ago. They told me it was sexually transmitted, but my husband didn't even have it."

She gasped. "Oh, really?"

"Yes. He said I must have gotten it from a nasty toilet. I thought I had been taking more precaution to prevent that fiasco from happening ever again."

Dr. Suarez clasped her hands together in a praying manner in front of her mouth and briefly closed her eyes. She blew out a deep breath before saying, "Janelle, it is not possible to contract Chlamydia from a toilet seat without some seriously disgusting effort, and even then, it would be questionable. There is no way for you to contract Chlamydia without your husband, unless you were stepping outside of your marriage. Even then, you would have given it to your husband, and he too would have tested positive. Men typically get symptoms within two days of contraction, but women can go for long periods of time without knowing they are positive. So, here is the scenario you are dealing with today: either you cheated on your husband or your husband cheated on you. Which is it?"

I felt like I was about to faint. How could I be so stupid and jeopardize my marriage like this—with Minister Hill? *Oh my lord, what am I going to do?*

After using up just about all of Dr. Suarez's tissues, I finally admitted, "I cheated on my husband. Oh my lord, how could I be so stupid? What was I thinking?"

"And your husband didn't mention any symptoms or burning in the past twenty-one days?"

"No, he hasn't mentioned anything."

"If you contracted it outside of your marriage, your husband would definitely have it if you've been with him since. Did you use any protection with your other partner?"

"A condom? Yes. Definitely. I wasn't even thinking about diseases, but he didn't know my tubes were tied. He didn't want to worry about any babies."

"You're sure there were no nips or tears in the condom? Was there any leakage?"

"None at all. I saw the condom after and there was a lot of stuff inside after he removed it. He even laughed about his collection of children trapped inside of the condom."

"Then it would seem your husband would be the culprit then. You're going to have to talk to him either way. You can't be treated without him being treated as well."

"So you're saying this happened within the past twenty-one days? Because I just can't imagine. Derrick has been a superstar husband this past month. Now the months before were questionable, but not this one."

"No, the reason I said twenty-one, is because it can sometimes take up to twenty-one days to even test positive. You could have had it longer, since you weren't tested for it during your last two visits. You were checked six months ago, and it was negative then."

"Is it possible that I could have given it to him? That was about a month ago that I cheated on him that one time."

"Anything is possible, but it's highly doubtful that your husband wouldn't have noticed the symptoms. However, I will say this in your husband's defense; you really have no right going off half-cocked on him, when you are just as guilty of violating the marriage. Maybe it's time for you two to get some marriage counseling and decide if this is a marriage worth saving. Whatever you do, don't call yourself saving it for the children. That never ends well. But whatever the case, you have to tell him and let him know that this disease is not the result of any toilet seat. I can bet you that he didn't even get angry when you had it before, did he?" Dr. Suarez asked, shaking her head.

I was getting angrier by the millisecond. First, as much as I love a tell-it-like-it is doctor, how dare she judge me so harshly? She didn't know half of what Derrick put me through. Nonetheless, as much as her words stung, she was absolutely right about me now being just as guilty. Second, the more I thought back to that first Chlamydia experience, Derrick wasn't the least bit angry, nor did he accuse me of any wrongdoing.

"No. No, he didn't. He wouldn't touch me for about a month, but he wasn't angry."

"I'm surprised your last doctor allowed you to believe that toilet seat nonsense, when your husband has been jeopardizing your life like that. It could have been something untreatable. You should have been in counseling back then to get to the root of your problems. Stepping outside of your marriage is NOT the answer to your problems. How did that foolishness work out for you? Did it fix the problems in your marriage, or did it make you feel worse?"

"Worse. Definitely, worse. I still feel stupid."

"As you should," she scolded. "Now, I highly suggest you get that counseling scheduled right away. Trust me, the conversation about Chlamydia doesn't often go too well, especially not in marriages."

"So you're saying he really, without a doubt, is cheating on me, and has been cheating on me? It's not my imagination or insecurities?"

"Janelle, you cheated on your husband. You are equally as guilty, so keep that in mind. Now, I am sending over a prescription to your pharmacy for the Chlamydia, and I want to see you back here in about a month so we can recheck your Chlamydia and fibroids. With regards to the fibroids, I don't think it would be good to stop the hormone treatment at this point since it's doing what it needs to do. Oh, and I'll be running another toxicology on you again, and if it comes back positive again, I will be sending you to drug counseling."

I couldn't believe I was being accused of being a drug addict. I would never use any of that stuff. Surely it had to be a mistake.

I don't know why I felt compelled to call Kenny with the play-by-play details of my life and marriage. Perhaps if I had a therapist or counseling, I would have someone else to talk to. But after attempting to make an appointment and being told the first opening was more than six weeks away, I had to settle for Kenny as my interim counselor.

"Kenny, I'm going to kill him!"

"Oh lord, what has my big brother-in-law done now?" He chuckled.

"He's about to be your *dead* big brother-in-law."

"It can't be that bad—definitely no worse than all of the other drama. As a matter of fact, from this day forward, I'm changing your names from Big Sis and Big Brother-in-law to Drama King and Drama Queen. Y'all sure keep it going. Y'all need a reality television show, just for the two of you—oh, and the kids."

I wanted to laugh. Typically, I'd laugh, but today was no laughing matter, and he noticed.

"Uh-oh! No laughing today? What's really good, Big Sis?"

"I now have proof that my husband is cheating on me and has been cheating on me since we were living in Nashville. I can't believe how stupid I've been."

"No, stupid was when you cheated on him, as if that would fix all of your problems—with your minister of all people. Ugh! But anywho, why are you looking for proof? What's going to change? You said he's finally being the husband you've wanted and needed, so, what, now you're going to go rock the boat with your proof? I say leave it alone and put it behind you. You've worked so hard to get to this point, with my fashion help, of course." Kenny laughed.

"I have Chlamydia, and now I must tell him," I blurted out into the phone before crying again.

"Whoa! TMI! TMI! So, you caught it from the reverend? Girl, didn't you use a condom?"

"I did use a condom. I got it from my husband again."

"Again? What do you mean, *again*? How could you have it before and not be sure your husband was cheating on you?"

"I didn't know for sure. He claimed he didn't have it and I must have picked it up from a toilet seat or something. I didn't understand, but I believed him. I know I had never been with anyone else."

"Please tell me you didn't fall for that toilet seat nonsense, sis."

"I did. Today my doctor told me he's a pathological liar, so now you see why I want to kill him. And the timing couldn't be worse."

"Why is that? No time is a good time."

"Yesterday I purchased this beautiful pink Kahr P380. It was so pretty. It called me as I walked past the gun store window."

"Janelle Desiree Roberts! You didn't!"

"Desiree? Who is that?" I asked confused.

"I don't know. A middle name just added to the theatrics. You know I don't know your middle name." He laughed.

I finally laughed as well. "Lil Bro, you are a serious nut. I thought I needed help, but you might have me beat."

"Well at least you're finally laughing. My job is done."

"No it's not. I don't know what to do. How am I supposed to confront him about this Chlamydia lie and refrain from shooting him at the same time?"

"First of all, you're going to take that gun right back to the store. Tell them they failed to run a psychological test on you, and for that reason, your lil bro is insisting you return the gun. Once the gun is no longer a threat, you will sit your husband down, privately, and nicely let him know he cheated on you and gave you Chlamydia, not once, but twice, and it didn't come from any toilet seats, now or in the past. Tell him that you are willing to forgive him if he admits his wrongdoing and stop with the lies, since you have been doing so well with the marriage. Now, if he insists on denying it, tell him that you have good grounds for a divorce, and it will be an ugly, bank-breaking ordeal if he wants to keep trying to play you for the fool."

"I don't know if I can forgive him. He really made a fool of me."

"No, Big Sis, you made you the fool. You chose to buy that toilet seat nonsense and even more so, it was you who slept with the reverend to get back at your husband for what you didn't even know to be true at the time. But worse than anything, I'm really going out on a limb by saying it was your husband that gave you the disease and not the reverend. I heard you say you used a condom, but babies have been made with condoms on. You don't even know for one-hundred percent certain that it was your husband, but still, I would approach the situation as if you knew for certain."

"What about when we were in Nashville? There was no one else then," I asked, wanting Kenny to be more on my side.

"We are in the here and now. Stop dwelling on that to make yourself feel more justified about your misdeeds. And I know you don't want to hear me fuss at you again, but sleeping with a pastor is like one of the most reprehensible, degrading acts ever. That's even lower than your husband sleeping with all the women in the church."

"It wasn't the pastor, it was the pastor's son, Minister Hill," I tried to defend. I hated when Kenny yelled at me. He was right, but I hated how low he made me feel. I was already feeling low.

"Girl, don't make me hang up this phone on you. Same disgusting thing! Now, all I'm trying to say is, find some compassion to forgive him if he's willing to own up to his doings and do not bash him over the head with it. You have absolutely no right to do that. Now what about this scenario? What if your husband hasn't been with anyone and you gave the disease to him? How do you plan on handling that?"

Oh! Gee! I hadn't considered that possibility. I knew that would be a true tragedy.

"I guess I'd tell him I got it from the toilet seat again. What, you think he'd tell me I was lying this time, but I somehow got it that way when he suggested it?"

"Oh lord! You two deserve each other. I gotta go. We have work to get done. Oh, but before I go, any word about that credit card statement you caught?"

"No, no other statements came here, but perhaps I'll try to see what I can get online. I keep intending to, but then get sidetracked."

"Oh, okay. But, sis, on this final note, please take that gun back. You and a gun is like C4 and a terrorist. That's a deadly mix. I'm not trying to be called to testify at your trial. You won't get me to lying, so take it back, A-S-A-P!"

"Fine! I'll take it back." I chuckled. "Love you, Lil Bro."

"Aww, I'm feeling special. Let your husband hear you saying you love some other man, and that crazy nightmare might get really-real, real soon." Kenny laughed.

"Yeah, right." I laughed, agreeing. "Never mind."

"No take back'sies now, dag-nab-it! I said I was feeling special. How you gonna try to take it back? I just said don't be letting the Drama King hear, and be inviting drama in my innocent world."

"Okay, I got it. Bye, Lil Bro."

"Bye, Drama Queen."

I smiled after hanging up from Kenny, as I often did, but my insides were churning some kind of fierce. I certainly wasn't looking forward to my inevitable conversation with Derrick.

Chapter 33

decided to take an alternative route to tackle my Chlamydia issue before discussing it with Derrick or beginning my treatment. Five days had passed and still no complaints of symptoms from Derrick. Sadly, things had been going so great with us and the household that it pained me to rock the boat.

I went to see Minister Hill and explained my dilemma to him. At least I knew he couldn't get angry with me. Although he assured me that he had no symptoms, he also went to see his doctor and produced a copy of his negative results. Although there was no name, but only a patient number, I found it funny that Derrick never showed me any report when he told me his results were negative that first time. I was so angry from seeing that men also are given paper results, contrary to what Derrick told me. I was half tempted to let Minister Hill "pray" over me again while he hammered away at my husband's infidelity. This probably had something to do with his sudden decision to find us a new church. I refrained, as I heard Kenny yelling in my head. I also refused any beverages or food from Minister Hill, just in case he was the reason I tested positive for drugs.

Later, when I was able to get Derrick in the bedroom after the kids went to bed, I found my nerve.

"Derrick, I know you call me insecure when I accuse you of being unfaithful, but as per your request, I went to see my doctor a few weeks ago about possible side effects of my hormone pills, and to my surprise, she told me that my fibroids are doing so well from the pills, I might eventually be able to completely forego surgery if I just stay the course."

I could see the confusion in his face. He was smiling, but his eyebrows looked confused.

"Wow! That's great! So you're telling me I only have to deal with a nutty wife for a little while longer?" He laughed.

I smiled. "I guess."

"I think I can manage. After all, you've put up with my madness for so long, I think it's the least I could do for my beautiful wife."

I was blushing. I was about to lose my nerve, but I knew it had to be done. I couldn't live the rest of my life with Chlamydia just to avoid telling him, 'cause lord knows I had considered it until I read about the long term effects on the internet.

"Well, there's more."

"More good news?" he asked, looking excited.

"No, that was it for the good news."

He frowned.

I continued. "During my visit, the doctor ran a bunch of tests and found that I have Chlamydia again." As I was speaking, anger was overtaking me and tears formed in my eyes. "I have it AGAIN, Derrick!"

He sat on the bed with that stupid "What did I do?" look.

"I don't understand. Are you saying I have done something wrong?" he foolishly asked.

He looked so pitiful, I almost felt sorry for him. But I continued my battle. "Derrick, you slept with some nasty, diseased woman, AGAIN, with no protection, AGAIN, and again, you brought home a disease—a sexually transmitted, not-from-a-toilet-seat disease. If cheating on me wasn't bad enough, but you did it with no protection, no regard for my life or our family, and even worse, you tried to make it as if I was crazy for thinking you were cheating on me. The pills aren't what's making me crazy. It's you and these silly games you play with my mind and emotions, and now my body and my life. I let you convince me that I caught Chlamydia from a toilet seat, even when I knew better. You wouldn't even take responsibility or ask forgiveness. Instead, you treated me as if I were the one in the streets, whoring around. You punished me for your selfishness. So I can't wait to hear how you'll rationalize this faux pas."

"Janelle, wow! I am sorry. I'm sorry you have some disease that you feel I gave to you, but I promise you, I haven't been with any other woman. No, I haven't always treated you as kind as I should, but I would not do that to you or our marriage. But is what I'm hearing you say to me, is that I need to go to the doctor to be treated for a sexually transmitted disease?" he asked calmly.

"Oh, so now you're going to play like it's my imagination again? Or are you insinuating that I get off rubbing up on nasty toilet seats?"

"I don't know how you got it, but I assure you, it was not me."

I couldn't take the lies anymore. I paced back and forth, fighting the urge to go into my closet to retrieve the pretty pink gun Kenny made me promise to return. Derrick was not taking ownership or responsibility.

"Derrick, my god! Please don't do this. I so desperately want to forgive you and move forward, but we can't move forward by sweeping lies underneath rugs. Not anymore. I can't do it."

He sat so stoic. "So what are you trying to say? You can't make me say something that isn't true."

"No, I can't seem to make you say anything that is true," I yelled.

"Please keep your voice down before you wake the kids."

"Okay, Derrick. If I just say let's go get treated and forget the whole thing, what do you have to say to that? I forgive you, so now we can move forward, okay?" I asked out of desperation.

"Well, I'm sorry you feel this is some simple situation that can be ignored so easily. Do you not think I am going to be always thinking about what you keep doing to get this disease? That's not something I can just ignore again."

NO HE DID NOT! He had the nerve to be turning this back on me. How dare he!

I took a seat on the foot of the bed, and sat on my hands. Oh yeah, I was that close to killing him.

"I want a divorce. I'm done playing this game. I'm done trying to appease everyone. I'm done trying to prove my sister wrong about you. I'm done living lies— your lies."

"Fine," he casually answered.

I sure didn't expect that response, with no hesitation. "What do you mean, 'fine?'"

"Didn't you just say you want a divorce?"

"Yes."

"Okay, well, what don't you understand?"

"So you're willing to throw our marriage and family away, just like that?" I asked, now standing.

"That was your choice, your request, and your decision. I'm simply granting you your request. I'm tired of fighting. No matter what, in your eyes, I'll always be guilty of something, and now with this Chlamydia mess, I see we no longer have any trust or marriage worth fighting for. And if you're looking for some big payday from this divorce, just know that won't be happening. We can sell this house and you can have your split to go get whatever new home you want, but you won't be getting another dime."

I looked at him as if he had just bumped his head. Oh, he really must think I'm stupid. "Let me see if I got this right: you get to go out with different women, pick up diseases, bring them to me, and then think you get to leave this marriage with everything, while leaving me and the kids with nothing?"

"You won't have my children. You'll get to live your single life. Isn't that what you wanted? That's why you asked for a divorce, right?"

"You know good and well I don't want a divorce. I want you to own up to your wrongs. Take some responsibility for a change. Stop making me out to be the bad guy when you know you are as wrong as sin."

"Face it, Janelle. It's over. We tried and we failed. Now you can be free without me or any children."

"So help me god, Derrick, I will kill you. Don't you ever threaten to take away my children ever again. And if you want to leave, then leave, but you will pay—dearly. Trust me."

Derrick laughed. "We'll see."

He got up and left the room, presumably to go sleep in another room. I couldn't remember all Kenny told me to say, but I didn't recall the plan having it end like this—with me as the villain.

Chapter 34

Derrick had been gone for a week. He told the kids he was taking a business trip but told me nothing. I didn't know if he just needed a little time and space to clear his head, but I certainly realized I wasn't ready to throw the towel in on my marriage. I definitely wasn't ready for the call from my mother.

"I knew it! I knew it! You finally did it. You weren't going to be happy until you destroyed your marriage," she scolded as quickly as I answered.

"Momma, what are you talking about?"

"I spoke with Derrick. Poor baby is so devastated. You got the man scared to go home, talking about you're going to kill him."

"He threatened to take my kids from me, and he's the one doing wrong."

"Who told you he's doing you wrong? All those people you tell your business to? That man hasn't done anything, but you insist on punishing him."

I choked from disbelief. "Punishing *him*! Are you serious? Are you confusing him with me? He's punishing me now. He's been gone a whole week all because I confronted him about giving me a sexually transmitted disease for the second time. All I wanted him to do was admit his wrong so I could forgive him and we could move on from it."

I cried. I cried hard. I was so broken up about losing my husband. Little did anyone know, right at that moment, I'd take him back without any further discussion on the infidelity.

Momma was actually quiet for a change.

"Momma, I don't know what to do. I don't want to lose my family. I had to tell him about the Chlamydia so he could be treated along with me. I would have forgiven him. As stupid as it may sound, I would have forgiven him. I love my husband, Momma. Do you hear me? I love him."

"I hear you, baby," she said in a soft, loving tone. "I wish you would have called me before you spoke with him. I would have told you to put the medicine in his food and drink." She paused to take a deep breath. "I had to do that with your daddy more times than I care to remember. Eventually, all stray dogs find their way home."

"Momma! Daddy?" I couldn't believe what I was hearing.

"And you see where he's still at, forty-five, almost forty-six years later. Listen to me, girl. I know you haven't done anything wrong, and I know how much your family means to you, but you're going to have to bite the bullet on this one. Tell him you were wrong for accusing him and make up something crazy of how you got it. You tell him you were wrong for threatening him and saying you want a divorce, and then you're just going to have to wait out the storm. It might be a month or two, but he'll see you are trying, especially since the old rascal knows he did you wrong. He knows good and well that you didn't give him any disease, no matter how much he tries to lie about never being with anyone else.

"I could tell he wasn't ready to end the marriage when he called to talk to me. He was asking for advice on how to deal with your threatening to kill him, and he mentioned that you were sleepwalking and doing crazy things in your sleep. He said you have to keep taking those pills because they are working, but he said he's afraid for his and the kids' lives."

"I had a bad dream one time. Ironically, it was about him confessing to me about all the women he's slept with as he held a gun to my head. In the dream, he accused me of cheating on him with my business partner, and then told me I had to go stand in the corner so he could beat me with his belt.

"Even when he asked me to recall my dream, I told him I couldn't remember, because I was so worried about upsetting him with my insecurities.

I have never had that happen again. I spoke with my doctor and she assured me it had nothing to do with my hormone pills, which was the reason I went to the doctor in the first place—upon his request."

"Yeah, I hear you. I don't like it either, but you are a good wife, Janelle, and don't let anyone tell you differently."

Those were shocking words coming from the one person who constantly reminded me of how poor I was as a wife, and the same one who once accused me of cheating with Kenny.

"Thank you, Mom. I really needed to hear you say that."

"Oh, and by the way, you better stop screaming divorce every time you get upset. He said this wasn't the first time you said it. Men don't like living in contentious homes. Read your Bible."

"I'll read more, and I have definitely learned my lesson about screaming *divorce* when things don't go my way."

Although the words were coming from my mouth, I couldn't help but roll my eyes at the whole notion about my having to learn my lesson. I also wanted to question my mom on the scriptures in the Bible that allow divorce for adultery, but since I knew I too had sinned and I didn't really want a divorce, I decided to keep quiet. The crazy thing is, the hardest part of letting Derrick go was the thought of him leaving me for Carmen or Jocelyn. Also, the battle over my children. I couldn't imagine them appreciating me enough to tell a judge that they'd want to live with me instead of Derrick. But then again, it would have been nice to see Derrick get a whiff of what life was really like for me.

After I got off of the phone, I suddenly remembered that I was supposed to be investigating the credit card statement. I had to be prepared just in case Derrick chose to finalize our marriage. I needed to see where all our assets were spread out.

Hacking his account was fairly easy, being I had all of his identifying information. I was just kicking myself for not thinking of doing it sooner. The current statement showed a $1,200 purchase at Babies-R-Us. Of course Brittany immediately came to mind. Then there was a $1,600 payment to SM

Management. When I Googled the company, it was a property management company based in Louisville, KY, but had residential and commercial properties in Chicago, Louisville, Memphis, Atlanta, and Cleveland. There were some payments to different technology companies, a payment to Home Depot, a payment to Walmart, and another grocery store charge for $250.

I had to log off, as I felt like I was the verge of a heart attack. I called Kenny with my findings and told him I suspected Derrick was paying rent someplace, probably for his love nest, since there were no hotel charges. It really made no sense that Derrick would be purchasing any baby items for Brittany, since her family already lived extravagantly. She never asked me for any help with getting anything for her pregnancy or the upcoming baby.

Kenny advised me to stop digging for evidence of wrongdoing if I was planning on taking Derrick back or fighting for my marriage. I agreed to back off.

It was another four days before Derrick decided to return home. The kids were so excited. Deep down, so was I, but those credit card purchases were making it very difficult to show any enthusiasm.

After the kids went to bed, I recited my mother's words of humility to him. He acted nonchalant, but he actually slept in the same bed with me. He didn't attempt to touch me, nor did he actually speak to me. He'd just stare at me, shake or nod his head, answer with an "Interesting," or occasionally chuckle. Personally, I think I did a phenomenal job. Momma would have been proud to call me her own, had she witnessed my stellar performance.

Surprisingly, only two days later, my husband was back to making love—scratch that—back to having sexual relations with me. He still hardly spoke to me, but it seemed like we were making progress. That is, until Julie let me know that Derrick was going to be away for a business trip he didn't bother to mention to me.

Chapter 35

I was on the verge of tracking down Derrick's little love nest and showing up with the kids so that his scandalous behind could be exposed once and for all. Of course I had to call Kenny to share my plans, and he had to talk me off the ledge yet again. He made my day when he suggested I find a babysitter for the evening and meet up with him and some friends for a happy hour. He said he was going to build up a whole financial and business development team since he had more business than he could accommodate.

My dilemma: A babysitter.

I already knew that the middle-aged woman we chose for a new babysitter was away attending to her recently deceased father's affairs. It pained me to think about calling Brittany while suspecting her of being with my husband intimately. But the thought of an evening out on my own was just too exciting to pass up.

"Hi, Brittany. How are you?"

"Hi, Miss Janelle. We are doing great. The baby is getting so big. I can't wait until he gets here."

"You still have a few more months, don't you?" I asked.

"Yes, ma'am. It's not soon enough for me. Oh, I heard you guys changed churches. Grandma was so disappointed. I think maybe you should call her sometime. She really liked you. She never likes anyone."

I smiled, thinking about Mother Hill, but then another more pressing thought entered my mind. "So, have you started getting things prepared for the baby yet? I'm sure you need a lot of stuff."

"Yes, ma'am. I have so much stuff already. That's why I can't wait. This boy is going to be spoiled when he gets here. Between my family and my fiancé—"

"Your fiancé? I didn't know you got engaged. That is wonderful."

"Yes, ma'am," she said yet again. "Hopefully we'll be married soon."

"Well, congratulations, Brittany."

"Thank you, Miss Janelle."

"Anyhow, I was calling to see if you'd be available for a couple of hours this evening. I have an important business function to attend, and Derrick's out of town."

She hesitated before answering. "Oh, I'm sorry, Miss Janelle, but I'm supposed to spend the night with my fiancé, and he said he doesn't want me babysitting anymore because he doesn't want anything to happen to our baby. He's very protective." She giggled.

I wanted to ask if she had finally figured out who her baby-daddy was, since her first accusation didn't go over so well.

"I understand, but thanks just the same. And don't forget to invite me to the wedding and the baby shower."

She was so giddy. "I won't forget. I'll make sure you have a front row seat next to my grandma. How's that?"

"Sounds great!" I said half-sincere. To be honest, I wasn't the slightest bit interested in her, her baby shower, or her so-called fiancé. However, I was interested to see the fool she pinned this baby on. Someone would have to be stupid to marry her while she was unsure of her baby's paternity.

Yeah, I was definitely disappointed about not having a babysitter. I wanted to call our former babysitter, Kathy, but she stopped answering my calls long ago. I always wondered what happened with her. And my dream of Derrick telling me he slept with her only fanned the flames of my colorful imagination. So I had to let Kenny know I couldn't make it. I was so disappointed that I was reconsidering that divorce and my ability to have the freedom to leave Julie in charge sometimes.

Instead, I was transporting the boys to their karate practice while I took Julie and her friend, Sandy, to the nail salon next door to the karate school for a mani-pedi. There was an empty space in that same strip mall that I often eyed, for the possibility of maybe actually opening up my own office someday. The location was great and it was in the same area I had to come to for the karate lessons, the music lessons, and the nail salon. There were even a couple of nice shops I'd shop for the kids in. I was so tired of my dreams being deferred. Someone had leased the space; I think just to taunt me. It'd been a couple of months now and they hadn't even opened yet. They hadn't even put up a sign. Yeah, I think someone saw me watching it too much and wanted to put me out of my misery of believing that could be my very own office someday.

As I cruised through the parking lot looking for a good spot to park, my thoughts were all over the place. I was angry. Angry that I could not go to happy hour and enjoy my life.

I started thinking about how Brittany knew we had changed churches, when I had only mentioned it to Minister Hill. I wondered if he told his family I came to see him. If so, did Brittany get word back to Derrick? He acted so convinced I was the one who cheated on him. Then, I thought about my nightmare, coupled with the memory of smelling my perfume in the guest bedroom, mixed with Derrick's cologne. I couldn't help but think of that $1,200 Babies-R-Us charge, and I wondered if that was Derrick spoiling "his" baby—a son.

I remembered back to the time when I had to go see about Daddy, and Brittany was there fixing meals for the kids. I thought back to that first time I left Brittany and Derrick in the house alone, and how he slept in the basement, where I found that stretched condom. I thought about the insurance policy, that he probably bought to have me and the kids knocked off, so he could get the money and marry Brittany and raise their baby, while they had nonstop sex.

I thought about how Derrick got to live his life and have his fun at Jocelyn's house, with near-naked girls all over him. I thought of Derrick enjoying his life, eating Carmen's fish . . . and other goodies.

I thought of how I hadn't had a chance to get to the gun range in a while, since getting all of those new clients.

I thought of Ol' Willard Barker, and how I could pay him back for disrupting my peace when I was at the gun range.

But then I remembered the pretty pink Kahr P380 I had been riding around with under my seat, debating if I would actually return it as I told Kenny I would.

Chapter 36

The kids were so loud and annoying, cluttering up my already cluttered thoughts. Julie sat up front with me, going on and on about her upcoming soiree, while she yelled over the music she insisted on playing to have conversation with Sandy, who was seated behind me. Byron and Bryce had their ongoing competitive conversations. But as I was driving through the large parking lot, I spotted Derrick and Brittany, appearing to be coming from the maternity store, looking like they were in love. They were laughing, probably at me. They were both carrying bags at first, but then Derrick, being the gentleman that he was, took the bags from Brittany. She turned and hugged him. I saw the flash of a diamond from her left ring finger when she placed her hand on Derrick's face.

Then I heard gossiping Sandy yell out, "Oh my goodness, Julie! Isn't that your dad over there kissing that girl, Brittany? Eew! And she's pregnant. Oh man, check out that huge rock she's sporting."

I heard Byron giggle, "Ooh, Daddy's cheating on Mommy!"

Then Sandy yelled one of her famous sayings for when she sees something scandalous or media worthy, "Worldstar!"

During all the loud excitement, I heard Julie yell, "Mom! Do something! Do you know how embarrassing this is? People are going to clown me! Aren't you going to say something?"

I really didn't remember much from that point. Something took over me. I could no longer hear any of the kids, nor the music, as I watched my husband all cozy with his teenaged fiancée and baby-momma. I spotted Derrick's car and realized they were headed there. I could hear Julie's words screaming in my head, to do something. I repeatedly heard Byron yelling and laughing that Daddy was cheating on Mommy. I kept hearing, "Worldstar!"

I didn't remember telling the kids to get out of the car, nor do I remember them doing so. I remember Derrick looking directly at me, smiling—possibly laughing, standing at his opened trunk with Brittany, as they deposited the bags. Even Brittany was looking at me smiling or laughing as I accelerated with everything in me. Their eyes went from laughter to terror as they watched me get closer. Derrick wrapped his arms around Brittany from behind, adding gasoline to my exploding mind, but it was too late.

The front rail of my 4Runner hit them both. I reversed to hit them again, but Derrick's body fell to the side of his car, leaving me to hit just Brittany. I reversed again, but then remembered the gun that I had hidden underneath my seat, which had slid up against my foot. I got out of the car and went and shot Brittany in the stomach, since she was still reaching her hand out to me. Then I saw the ring again and shot her repeatedly then snatched the ring off. Surely my money paid for it. I shot until there were no more bullets. And then I kept hitting her in the face with the gun. At first I heard pure silence, but suddenly my hearing returned, and I heard screams and sirens, causing me to see the mess I had just made. It was like I was in a trance. I dropped the gun to the ground and stood with a bloody hand over my mouth as I realized the horror show I had just stepped into. As the police cars surrounded and other police approached me with their guns drawn, confused, I was able to see my traumatized children standing on the curb along with my parents, Derrick's parents and siblings, JJ, Janae, Deacon Farmer, Kenny, and a few other people, to include two of my clients. Everything happened so fast, and next thing I knew, I was being taken away in the back of a squad car, for all of the Worldstar audience to see.

For the life of me, I couldn't understand why our families, Kenny, my clients, and the sixty-year-old widowed Deacon Farmer from Pastor Hill's church were there. Surely, it must have been my imagination. Then I began to wonder if everything was my imagination. Did I really see Derrick and Brittany making out after coming from the store? Why were the kids out of the car when I had just heard them screaming at me? Was Sandy really in the car recording for Worldstar? Was I sleepwalking again or having another bad dream? It had to be . . . right?

Chapter 37

Roberts, your lawyer's here. Not that it'll do you any good, since you won't be going to see the judge tonight," Detective Shore yelled into the interrogation room where I had sat deliriously handcuffed to the table for what seemed an eternity.

Almost a day had gone by, and I hadn't awakened from this nightmare yet. I was actually locked up, praying for a ten-minute nap. How could I be dreaming, wanting to take a nap? I knew one thing, when I woke from this nightmare, I was going to take Derrick's advice and immediately stop taking those hormone pills. I didn't care if they were helping my fibroids. I could no longer deal with these side effects.

A well-dressed, obviously, high-paid attorney came into the interrogation room. "Uncuff her NOW!" he demanded as he slammed his attaché case on the table. "Has she been cuffed like this since yesterday?"

No one answered as they quickly obliged.

"Mrs. Roberts, I am your attorney, Jacob Schwartz. I've been hired by your family to represent you in the case of the murder of Miss Brittany Hill and her unborn child."

I was confused. They said I ran over Brittany and Derrick. Was Mr. Schwartz not going to represent me in the murder of Derrick?

"What about Derrick?" I asked, still hoping it was all a dream.

"Mr. Roberts doesn't want to press charges against you, but the state has their own agenda. They're going to try to prosecute without him, but they're more interested in the capital murder case. Mr. Roberts said that you'd been experiencing some psychological and medical problems lately, as a possible side effect to some kind of medication you've been on."

I was really confused. "Derrick's trying to help me after I tried to kill him?"

"Mr. Roberts and your parents hired me. They wanted the best money could buy, and they got me. I flew in from Chicago this morning. This was the soonest I could get here. I practice in three states, to include Tennessee. I've been practicing law for twenty-three years. I spent time as a prosecutor and a judge before going into private practice. I've been a defense attorney for twelve years and have only had three convictions in that time. I don't plan on having a fourth conviction . . . ever."

Now I knew I must be dreaming. In all of the television shows I've ever watched, I couldn't imagine anyone, other than God, Himself, being able to get me free of this horrific act.

I started laughing hysterically, and then walked over to the two-way mirror. "This is a nightmare, right? None of this is real. It can't be."

Mr. Schwartz looked at me with great concern. "I'm afraid you are not dreaming, Mrs. Roberts. This is real. Do you know where you are right now?"

I kept laughing, "This is not real and you are not real. I don't know how to wake up, but I don't like this dream. Help me wake up, please," I pleaded before crying.

Mr. Schwartz went to the door and knocked. When an officer opened it, he stepped out of the room and I could hear him yelling. When he came back, he said, "Mrs. Roberts, you're going to be transported to the hospital to get some rest and a psychiatric evaluation. I will be by to see you in the morning."

I sat back in my seat. "Okay, if you say so. So will you be back after I get some rest? How are you going to come back once I wake up? If this is a dream, and I wake up, then that means you and all of this will go away."

"Mrs. Roberts, you have been sleep deprived. You've been here for fifteen hours, cuffed to a table. You are not in your right mind. We need you to get some rest so we can start working on your case before you have to see the judge."

"Did I really kill Derrick and Brittany?" I asked, still having difficulty processing my life. "Did I really run them over, or was that a dream?"

"Mr. Roberts was badly injured, but he's in stable condition. He's still alive. Unfortunately, Miss Hill and her baby were killed when you ran them over and then shot and beat her. Hopefully, you'll help me understand everything after you get some rest."

"This can't be real, because I saw my parents, my in-laws, my siblings, my business partner and clients all there while it was happening. I even saw Deacon Farmer. My parents live near Nashville. Why would everyone be there if it were real?"

Mr. Schwartz had a grim look on his face. "Wow! This is really not good. You are really having difficulty processing reality."

I cried again. I was frustrated with my condition. I wanted to be home in my bed. I wanted to wake up.

He continued. "Mrs. Roberts—Janelle, your husband planned a surprise party for you at your new office. Your daughter was supposed to get you to the office you had wanted for a long time, but you thought someone else bought. Your husband bought the office for you, spent months fixing it up with the help of Miss Hill, and then they planned the surprise grand opening for the day they knew you'd be there to take your sons to their karate practice. Your business associate, Mr. Waldron, was in on the surprise party and had some of your clients there to greet you in your new office."

I was stunned—beyond shocked—but still none of it made any sense.

"But I saw Brittany and Derrick making out. Ask the kids. Even they saw it. How? Why? She said she was going to be with her fiancé that evening and couldn't babysit for me. I saw the ring. I remember taking it from her hand. She was going to have a baby with my husband and they were going to be married. I saw them together. He was all over her. He was hugging and kissing on her in front of our children." I said, getting louder and angrier as I cried.

"Janelle, I assure you, they were not making out. Your whole family was there waiting and watching for you to arrive. Miss Hill's fiancé, Mr. Farmer, was also in attendance for your event. He was there and witnessed his fiancée and child being killed. Miss Hill's grandmother was also waiting inside the office."

I couldn't take anymore. I passed out. I dropped to the floor. I was too overwhelmed.

I came to in a hospital bed. I felt like I slept for a whole day or more. I was sure I'd wake up to realize everything was a bad dream. Once I saw Mr. Schwartz walk into my room, I knew my nightmare wasn't over.

"Mrs. Roberts, hope you're fully rested, because we have a few problems."

"I was hoping when I was fully rested that you would no longer be real."

"Well, that might be a reality sooner than you think. Your husband's ready to pull the plug on my retainer, based on some new information that came to light while you were resting. Do you know a Willard Barker, a private investigator?"

"Yes," I answered with hesitation and confusion, wondering what he had to do with anything.

"Well, according to Mr. Barker, you requested his services into investigating your husband, and when he refused, you resorted to going to the gun range to practice killing your husband. Mr. Kenny Waldron pretty much corroborated that you were going to the range and you then purchased a gun. He said you mentioned killing your husband, but he didn't think the threat was credible. He said he advised you to return the gun to the store and couldn't imagine why you'd be riding around with a loaded gun that you were returning."

I felt betrayed by my friend, but then he was only telling the truth. I opened my mouth to speak, but words couldn't form to come out. Somehow I knew Willard Barker would be a thorn in my side.

"Unfortunately, the police have those statements. Also, your husband informed me that you were having an affair and recently gave him a STD. Apparently, you spoke with your mother about it, and your mother blamed your husband for making you crazy and giving you a disease."

"He did give me a disease, but I wasn't planning on killing my husband. My husband wanted me to learn how to use the gun he purchased last year. At first I was against the whole gun thing. Then I went to the gun range so I could learn how to use it if ever necessary. I ran into Mr. Barker while there and he accused me of 'hubby practice' right before offering to give me private lessons. When I went to the gun range the first time, I found it to be a stress release. That's why I went several times after. I simply purchased the gun because I saw it in a store window as I was passing, and thought it was pretty. The timing was bad, because I found out about the STD a couple of days after getting the gun. You can check with my doctor. So I promise you, there was absolutely no connection."

"Your husband also said you threatened to kill him as well," Mr. Schwartz said, looking at me as if he was totally Team Derrick.

"I did say that when he told me he was going to take my children from me, after giving me a disease. I asked for a divorce, because I was so tired of living with his infidelity."

"You do know how bad this looks and sounds, don't you?"

I closed my eyes. I agreed, it sounded like a slam-dunk case for the prosecution.

"And what about the guy you were having an affair with? Your husband is completely positive that you had an affair and gave him the disease. He admitted that he cheated on you a few years ago and gave you the same disease, but said despite what you believed, he has never been with another woman since then. He also admitted to being in inappropriate environments and having inappropriate pictures on his phone and computer, but swears he has never crossed the line beyond that, making it impossible to have contracted any disease. So as your attorney, between you and I, never leaving this room, tell me about the man you were involved with before the prosecution digs it up first and uses it as a motive for murder against you."

I cried. I was so embarrassed, hurt, and confused. How could I have gotten the disease if not from Derrick? I didn't want to have to confess about Minister Hill.

"Oh, and by the way, Mr. Waldron already told me the one person you told him about, but haven't told the state as of yet. Trust me, they are going to press the issue to help establish your premeditated motive. I need to see what type of relationship you and I are going to have. I believe I can convince your husband not to jump ship if I can convince him that the timing of the gun was coincidental, and the gun range was just to get the practice he wanted you to have for the gun he purchased."

"I swear, I had no intentions of cheating on Derrick at first. It was supposed to simply be lunch and prayer. I think I was drugged or something. Even my doctor said I was positive for some kind of substance that I know nothing about. I don't know how I ended up in a compromising position and doing what I did. He's one of the ministers at our former church. I remember the whole time how he kept telling me that Derrick was sleeping with all the women in the church, and then I remember not caring anymore. There was a condom used that one time, that I know about, and he also went to get tested before I confronted Derrick. I saw his paperwork. His tests were negative, and there was no one else but Derrick. Derrick wouldn't admit the truth, so I told him I wanted a divorce. I just wanted him to admit his wrong, apologize and then we could just move forward. He left me for almost two weeks. I knew then I couldn't live without him. I didn't care what he did. I was determined to fight for my marriage and family."

"But why kill Brittany, a pregnant woman who was your babysitter and friend? She helped your husband put together your big surprise. Supposedly, you mentioned to her how that office would have been like a dream come true.

She told your husband, along with your daughter, and they worked to get all of this for you. So everyone, including me, is confused as to why you'd want to hurt her."

"Brittany was having an affair with my husband. She slept with everyone's husband. She slept with teenaged boys, as well as old men. She didn't discriminate. When I was away, she'd wear my perfume for him, and then I'd smell his cologne and my perfume in the guest bedroom, on the pillow. In my own house."

"Is it possible they slept on the same pillow at different times?" Mr. Schwartz asked.

"I'm positive they've slept together. I found a stretched rubber down in the basement bedroom. I found a secret credit card statement with Victoria's Secret purchases, Babies-R-Us purchases, and some obvious rent payments to a company called SM Management."

Mr. Schwartz twisted his face and then said, "Did you know the property management company for your new office is SM Management? They're also headquartered in Chicago. My company does a lot of work with them."

Surely the color left my face. "So you're saying the rent payment was for my office?"

"I can't say for certain without seeing the charge amount and the paperwork, but it would be pretty coincidental. I don't know what the Babies-R-Us charges might be, but it's very possible that your husband could have been paying Miss Hill for coordinating your party and helping to decorate your new office—which I have to tell you, looks absolutely phenomenal. Too bad you didn't get to see it. It had plenty of high tech video conferencing to help you connect with your remote clients. There were pictures of your family, copies of your degrees and certification, as well as a fully stocked refrigerator. The place was great. It was personable, but still professional.

"Your husband swears he has not had any affairs since you lived in Nashville. He even told me who, and said that slip-up made him realize that unless he was ready to walk away from his family, he could never cross that line again. He said that was why he was willing to overlook your transgressions. He felt he deserved it. Even your hitting him with your truck, he felt he deserved that for making you so insecure with the women in the church who he said were very disrespectful to you. No one could understand why Brittany, though. Your daughter said you adored Brittany. She admitted that she didn't like Brittany at first, but when they started working on the office surprise, her feelings changed."

"Julie . . . Julie was in the car with me. She saw her father making out with Brittany. All the kids saw it," I said, getting excited. Surely, that was my proof I wasn't crazy or mistaken.

"Uh, no. No one saw what you claim to have witnessed. I'm not sure what you think you saw, but your daughter texted Brittany to let them know you guys were on your way and that you were angry because you wanted to go out somewhere but couldn't find a babysitter. Brittany responded with 'L-O-L' and said your surprise will be even better when you arrive. Your daughter then asked Brittany to tell your husband to remember to get her back-up outfits from her Aunt Denise, for her SS party, presumably her sweet sixteen. According to your husband, they were trying to hurry up and get the bags to the car before you arrived. They were all supposed to be inside the office when your daughter and her friend were to lure you there."

"But wait! I remember Sandy recording on her phone. I remember her saying, 'Worldstar' when she saw the pair."

"Sandy was recording because she was supposed to capture the whole surprise on video. Your daughter couldn't video because she was texting and she didn't want you to see her recording your expression. I have watched the video, and there is absolutely nothing inappropriate on it. Your husband took bags from Miss Hill right before they were going to step into the street. Mr. Roberts held his elbow out for Miss Hill to grab hold of, to keep her from falling, and then they walked to the car to put the bags in the trunk. That's when you hit them."

"NO! I saw them. I know what I saw," I yelled.

"Janelle, calm down! I will show you a copy of the video. There is nothing, I mean nothing damning on it. I think you just saw what you wanted to see because you already were thinking they were having an affair. I'm going to be back in a few hours and I'll bring a copy of it then. We have to get ready for your arraignment."

"What's that?" I asked. I was annoyed. I knew what I heard and saw. If that video showed different, then someone must have altered it. I didn't feel like arguing with my attorney. Derrick hired him for me, but he seemed like he was working for Derrick and justifying all of Derrick's lies.

"The arraignment is the first appearance before the judge, where your attorney goes on record and we state our intentions. The judge will then decide if there will be a bond or if a hearing would be required. I'd prefer to keep you in the hospital under psychiatric evaluation, rather than let you spend any time in the detention center. Trust me, this is like the Four Seasons compared to that place. Just keep your mouth shut and let me do all the talking. I'll tell you what to say and when to say it. You hear me?" he barked. He actually scared me more than the thought of a detention center.

He started walking to the door, and then I called out, "Hey, wait a minute!"

He turned back.

"You said you knew who my husband had an affair with. I want to know who it was."

"Do you want me to tell your husband who you had an affair with, although a trial will ultimately drag that out?"

"First of all, you work for me and not my husband, and second, why should I have to wait for a trial to find out who?"

Mr. Schwartz walked back to the door and then stopped to look back at me. "Why don't you ask your sister?" he said before he left.

Chapter 38

My attorney managed to keep me out of the detention center, but there was a dear price to be paid for that. I had to spend my time in a psychiatric hospital, being sedated around the clock. It was like when I was almost back in my right mind, it was time for my meds again. This was a part of Mr. Schwartz's grand scheme to keep me out of prison or being put to death.

I was allowed visits, but those didn't go too well. I was never coherent enough to speak or fully comprehend what was being said to me. I do remember seeing Derrick visit a few times, walking with a cane. The medicine could have been making me crazy, but I remembered him kissing me each time. It was like he really did love me. I wasn't well enough and didn't have the mental capacity to question him about my sister's involvement with his previous affair.

I recalled seeing Julie walk in one time, but then she left back out without any show of affection. My mom would come by and fix my hair and nails. I even remembered seeing Mother Hill. Even she kissed me in my memory.

As an eternity seemed to pass, the time for the trial came. Now while I already expected Willard Barker to be a witness for the prosecution, I wasn't expecting to see that my sister, Janae, and my only real friend and business associate, Kenny, would also be playing for the other team.

In the weeks leading up to the trial, Mr. Schwartz had the hospital staff turn down my meds so we could prepare for my trial. Even then, I was so hell-bent on talking about all of Derrick's affairs as the cause of me finally reaching my breaking point. There was nothing anyone could say that was going to convince me otherwise. That is, until Mr. Schwartz produced some subpoenaed documents, showing Minister Hill was indeed positive for Chlamydia. Even then, I argued the validity, because I clearly remembered Minister Hill showing me papers that he was negative. Mr. Schwartz was planning on putting Minister Hill on trial, saying that he drugs women to take advantage of them, and then was going to offer up scientific information of the adverse effects the combination would have on my hormone therapy. He even brought in my own doctor to discuss the traumatic effects of my medical condition and how they contributed to my mental instability. She testified about my positive toxicology report, and how I swore to her that I had never touched any drugs and assumed it must have been some mistake.

During the trial, Willard went on with his theories that I was at the gun range to kill my husband. He seemed credible, until my attorney team made mincemeat of him. By this time, my team included three attorneys and a paralegal. Willard's whole disgusting love life was played out for the court's viewing pleasure. Finally, he was exposed, because his wife decided to join him that day, and she learned that Ol' Willard had pretty much gone through every female in her family, to include a relationship he had with her mother many years ago, when she was too young to remember.

Kenny tried his best to be a good friend, but I obviously put him in a predicament by sharing my thoughts of killing Derrick and letting him know I purchased a gun. While the prosecution attempted to make our conversations sinister, my attorney made our conversations lighthearted and got Kenny to say that none of my concerns really surfaced until I stumbled across a large insurance policy, which caused me to be fearful for my life and those of my children. He said that was the point where I seemed to become paranoid and concerned that my husband was going to knock me off along with my children.

By the time Kenny finished testifying, I was feeling pretty confident with my chances of actually beating the charges against me. However, my sister—my dear sister, who always seemed to have my back, came along to put her knife in it. She testified that I was ALWAYS telling her how sick I was of Derrick's infidelity, and she added that I often spoke of killing him. None of which was true. She'd be the last person I'd say what I felt like to. I couldn't believe her outrageous lies, and I couldn't understand why she'd say things to help put me away for life. She added that she'd often tell me to get a divorce.

One of my attorneys got up after the prosecution finished questioning my sister and walked over to the jury, smiling at them before asking Janae, "At what point was your sister—your only sister, whom you claim to love so much—aware that you infected her husband with Chlamydia, a time when you seduced him in your sister's home, while she was away on a business trip for the day, just so you could convince her that he was cheating on her and she should leave him? Also, at what point did your sister feel a need to confide in you that she contracted Chlamydia from her husband, which in essence came from you? We'll wait," he asked as he went back to his seat and folded his hands in anticipation of her answer.

She couldn't get her words together to speak as the whole court gasped and I wailed out loud, refusing to believe she could be so conniving.

My second-chair attorney, Roger Daniels, was very animated and theatrical. If it weren't my own trial, I would love to sit and watch him in action. When Janae could do nothing but cry and swear she didn't mean it, Mr. Daniels went back over to the jury box and said to Janae, "So, in essence, it is YOU who should be sitting here on trial for trying to do all you could to use her medical condition of hemorrhaging and manipulating her mind that the world was out to get her, huh?" Before Janae could answer, he slid over to her and asked, "And exactly how were you helping the sister you claimed to love by infecting her with a venereal disease through her own husband, who you continually advised her to divorce?"

Janae cried out loud, "I'm so sorry, Janelle. I swear I was just trying to protect you."

Mr. Daniels continued. "Look at your sister. She's just as shocked as the rest of this court about your attempts to dismantle her marriage and family.

She had no idea about your involvement to sabotage her marriage. So I ask you, at what point did you do all of this confiding with one another, and at what point *ever*, did Mrs. Roberts let you know she had Chlamydia?"

Janae mumbled inaudibly.

Mr. Daniels yelled out, "I'm sorry, we were all having a very difficult time hearing you say, 'never.' Could you please repeat it for everyone to hear?"

She said it more audibly, but still low. "Never. She never said it. She never would confide in me. I knew he was a cheater and she wouldn't listen to me."

"And for what reason did you feel the need to come into this court and perjure yourself today?"

"I don't know!" she cried again. "I just thought if she went away, he'd love me and want to take care of me the way he does her." Janae stopped crying and switched to rage. "She doesn't deserve him. She'd rather bleed every day than make sure he's satisfied. He's a good man and she doesn't care if he's happy."

"So, sleeping around unprotected with random men and contracting diseases is your way of showing him that you're the better woman?"

"I didn't sleep around."

"It's a sexually transmitted disease!" Mr. Daniels yelled.

As good of a job he was doing at annihilating Janae, I was thoroughly embarrassed by my sex life being placed on trial.

"I was able to get some positive samples from the hospital lab I used to work in back then. I infected myself," she smugly admitted.

I stood up, slammed my hand on the table, and shouted, "You evil—" The attorneys at my table grabbed me and stopped me. I cried so hard, I didn't hear anything else she had to say. The court was adjourned for the day.

The prosecution team didn't have as much of a slam-dunk, premeditated case as they had hoped. After my dream defense team had pretty much pummeled the state's case, they went on to put on a medical team to make me sound so pathetic, I even felt sorry for my life.

My mother took the stand, telling everyone how she'd always tell me to stop telling all of my business. Not so helpful. My third attorney, Shelia

Walters, took on my mom, putting her prehistoric parenting skills on trial and accusing her of conditioning me to be docile until I snapped. She also rode my mother for causing me to believe that my medical condition was my own fault, coupled with Janae's constant suggestions of Derrick's infidelity. Ms. Walters made my mother cry, and that bothered me, even though her method was helping me win my case.

Derrick testified on my behalf and admitted sleeping with Janae that one time when we still lived in Nashville and told how he did all he could to avoid her since then. He testified that I had never seemed to have any issues with Brittany, and that he could understand how his actions on that day would be misinterpreted upon first sight. He admitted that he allowed the women from the church to cause me to become insecure during a time I was dealing with medical issues. He said he was frustrated and wanted me to do something about my condition. He told about the night he awoke and found me in a corner, naked and crying, unaware of my reality. He explained how he felt the finding of the insurance papers might seem alarming, but had often regretted not bringing them to me, rather than letting me find them. Then Derrick said something that blew my mind.

"I hear that there was talk about my wife going to the gun range to practice shooting me. That is far from the truth. I purchased a gun when we moved to Memphis, due to the increased crime rate. Janelle was very much against guns, and it was me who prodded her to get some practice, just in case it was ever needed. And that story about my wife trying to hire a private investigator for me is also not true. She wanted to hire one for her sister, but decided not to when she felt Mr. Barker's character was questionable. I convinced my wife to back off from investigating her sister, because I was afraid that my own misdeeds would come to light if her sister found out."

Mother Hill also came up on my behalf to tell how Brittany would be with any and everybody's husband, and she'd always warn her that it was going to get her killed one day. She told how Deacon Farmer's wife was still alive when Brittany conceived her child and then lied, saying it belonged to some young boy. Although she was sick for many years, his wife died from heart failure around the time word got out about sixty-year-old Deacon Farmer fathering Brittany's baby. Before the ink dried on the death certificate, he was already planning on marrying Brittany. The whole Hill family was against it, but since he was the supposed father, they went along with the engagement. A DNA test performed since their deaths revealed that he was not the father.

Of course, I am summarizing Mother Hill's testimony, 'cause lord knows, everyone struggled to comprehend the words she was saying.

Chapter 39

t took two days for the jury to return a not-guilty verdict based on temporary insanity. I couldn't believe I was heading home to get my life back . . . or so I thought.

Derrick picked me up from the hospital after I was processed out. He drove me to the place that was our home. It was dark, but out front sat a "For Sale" sign, with "Sold" placed over it. I was confused.

"What's this? What happened to our home?" I asked, ready to get out of the car to investigate.

"It's been sold. While you were declared mentally incompetent by the courts, I was able to get a power of attorney to sell the house to help pay your legal fees," Derrick calmly answered.

"But where are the kids?" I cried.

"The kids are fine. They are—we live in North Carolina now, near my parents' home. I took a new job at the university there. Surely, I couldn't stay here in Memphis after what you did. I can't begin to tell you the amount of trauma you have caused our children. And speaking of our children, I have full custody and we have a pending divorce. I'm hoping you'll just sign these papers and leave us alone," he said, holding up a large envelope.

"Oh—oh no! Absolutely not! Derrick, I was just found not guilty. It wasn't my fault. Why are you now punishing me? I thought you understood. You knew how I found that condom and credit card statement, making it look like you were having an affair. Mr. Schwartz explained the condom and statement to me. He said you were showing the boys what they looked like and how they must protect themselves when they got older. I believe you. And I believe you got that credit card for Julie, but also used it to help pay for my office."

"Janelle, you can sign these papers now and I'll take you wherever you want me to drop you off at, or you can get out right here and get where you need to on your own."

"Why are you doing this to me? To us? To our family? You said you understood. You just testified to help me. I don't understand. And where are my belongings?"

"Your belongings are at your parents', but since Janae was arrested for committing perjury in your trial, your mother doesn't want you in her home, particularly with you being a murderer and all. As for our family, you destroyed it. You go have an affair with that snake in the pulpit and then have the nerve to be plotting to kill me. I said what I said to help you. I felt somewhat guilty out of my frustration with you.

"I should have divorced you a long time ago, but I kept trying to hold on for the sake of my children. I got you that office because Julie told me you'd always go and peep in the window and called about the price. I thought maybe if you focused more on your business, you'd be more tolerable like you were in Nashville. I wanted to surprise you, as you now know. Holding onto this marriage has been a struggle for me—probably for you as well. I've had so many opportunities to be with other women and came dangerously close a time or two, but that one slip-up with Janae, as well as what came as a result, kept me from crossing the line since then. My family was more important.

"As for Brittany, no, she was not so innocent. She did attempt to seduce me, and yes, I have seen her naked body that she tried to entice me with. That was that first time she stayed over and I slept in the basement. I scolded her and she never did so again. She even apologized and cried, saying she's a bad person, mixed up in the head. I cautiously tried to help her get her life together, but then I learned she was pregnant and wasn't even sure by who. That was another thing that convinced me not to have any affairs, because I could have been caught up in that web of potential baby-daddies. After a while, she started getting her act together, and since she was often around you, I figured I could use her to help me get information to plan your office surprise. She managed to find some clown, happy to claim paternity, and even put a ring on her finger, hoping to make her an honest woman. You would have gotten to see she was with Deacon Farmer had you not killed her . . . and tried to kill me.

"So back to the point at hand. No, Janelle, we can no longer be together. I can't deal with your mental instability, also known as insecurities. You have proven to me just how dangerous you really are, and although I told the court that I sent you to the gun range, only you and I know that was a lie. I can't wrap my mind around why you'd withhold that kind of information from me, knowing I was trying to show you how to handle the gun I purchased for the house. So I am convinced that you had every intention to kill me on more than one occasion. I learned from your friend, Kenny, that he first saw me leaving a restaurant with a woman, and you were very upset then. Why'd you hide that?"

"Who was she?" I asked as if that mattered.

"Who was who?" he responded angrily.

"The woman. I saw your hand almost touching her bottom. You're trying to tell me there was nothing going on there?"

He looked at me like he was validating his conclusion that I was crazy. "Janelle, you're sick. Maybe you should be locked up. No one touched her nor her bottom. I guess you missed the man who walked out of the door first, carrying their newborn in a carrier. Her husband was supposed to be meeting me, but he decided to bring his family along for the ride so I could meet them.

"So out of all that I've just said to you, the only thing that stood out in your mind was the woman in the restaurant? Are you hearing me tell you that we are done—OVER?"

"But you just told me that Brittany did try to come onto you, so I wasn't that crazy, was I?" I asked, still not wanting to accept the demise of my marriage and loss of my children. "And what about all those business trips you would take? Am I supposed to believe you weren't having any affairs?"

"Janelle, please sign these papers and let me drop you off somewhere. JJ said you could stay with him in Atlanta for a while to get back on your feet. I could drive you to your parents' to pick up a suitcase and then take you to the airport. I'll do it if you sign these papers right now."

"You're going to bully me into a divorce? Why can't you answer me?" I asked before crying.

"No, I'm not trying to bully you. I could have withheld legal services and my false testimony, which helped keep you from prison, and I would have gotten my divorce with ease. So, now that I have helped you to have a life again, after taking two innocent lives and almost mine, I feel signing these papers is the least you could do. As for the business trips, some were legitimate and some were to just get away. Sometimes I'd feel like I was suffocating. I hated having a wife, but couldn't 'have' my wife because you were always bleeding—or just acting crazy. Contrary to what you may have believed, none of those trips involved any other women. If anything, they made me realize how much I needed you in my life, despite our poor sex life. Eventually, I started working on getting your office and having it fixed up, so I had to tell you it was business trips, then. I thought that would help us as a family."

"What about my children? You just want me to walk away from them?"

"Janelle, you need to go get your life in order before you see them. You murdered someone right before their very eyes. They watched you try to kill their father. Trust me, Julie wants nothing to do with you, and the boys have nothing but questions. This is not a conversation they need to have with you anytime soon. I also don't want them thinking it's okay to get away with murder, like you did."

"You think I am a murderer, Derrick?"

"There's no thinking about it. You are a murderer. You set out to kill someone simply because you thought I was involved with them. That makes you a murderer. If you wanted to kill someone, you should have knocked off that menace to society, that walking disease, Minister Hill—and from what I've heard from Carmen and Jocelyn, his father as well."

"I knew you were sleeping with them. I knew it!" I yelled in an ah-ha moment.

Derrick looked at me as if I was truly certified. "Janelle, for the last time, sign these papers so I could be rid of you for once and for all. If you don't, I'm going to drive you to the closest police precinct and drop you off there." He pushed the papers in my direction along with a pen. I contemplated stabbing him in the neck with the pen. I figured if I couldn't have him, no one would, and certainly not my backstabbing sister.

I took the envelope and pen and then asked, "How exactly did you end up sleeping with my sister of all people?"

He must have been reading my mind about the stabbing thing. "No more questions answered until I have both the pen and signed papers back in my possession.

I gave in and signed the papers, not without a mental delay about killing him. After I returned everything, he started the car again and pulled off. We were on the highway headed to Nashville before he chose to answer.

"You were so busy playing Superwoman for everyone else that you would be too tired for me. You'd make our sex life like one of the items on your to-do list. Janae and I were really cool. We used to talk a lot. I remember the kids were at your mother's and you were on some kind of business trip and not due back until late that night. Your mom sent Janae by with some food for me, as she had done many times before. We were sitting and talking, and next thing I knew, we were kissing. I started thinking that you'd either be bleeding or too tired for me when you got home, so I let it go all the way. I immediately felt bad about it. Ironically, you came home that night in full seduction mode. I was turned on, not giving any more thought to Janae. I was enjoying my frisky wife. A few days later, I started burning. As far as I knew, Janae wasn't seeing anyone, and for a hot minute, I thought maybe it was you who cheated. I couldn't say anything, so I had to find a way to avoid you. When I spoke with

Janae about it, that's when I learned that she's a hammer short of a toolbox. She told me she gave it to herself so you'd leave me and she and I could be together. She wanted you to raise the kids while she and I rode off into the sunset. I kept my distance after that. She'd often try to blackmail me, but I still managed to avoid her while alone. She is the reason I sought the position in Memphis. I knew we'd never be alone again. That time when she came to visit with your mother, she sent me a message while they were in transit, saying she couldn't wait to be with me again. I didn't really understand what that meant until you told me she was at the house, so I decided not to come home until they left. One day I received a message from her saying she found a way for us to be together even with everyone in the house and couldn't wait to show me. So that's when I started skipping family dinners. Eventually, I spoke with my parents about what I had done, which is why they started skipping as well."

"Why couldn't you just tell me the truth instead of letting our lives get to this? I would have forgiven you."

I was so angry, I could spit. Janae was telling me my marriage wouldn't last from the beginning. I guess that's what she was hoping the entire time.

"I wish I could've erased that day and made it never happen. She obviously set out to trap me that day. She infected herself, just to make you leave me."

"Yet, now you're throwing me away and giving her exactly what she wanted. So you could be with her?" I asked, crying yet again.

"Now there's too much damage, Janelle. I would have forgiven your affair, because of what I had done. Especially with me now knowing that creature had the nerve to drug my wife. Eventually, I would have sat down with you and we could have both come clean, but you killed someone and intended to kill me as well. I can't overlook that. I'll always be afraid of what crazy thoughts are swirling around in that pretty head of yours, and you'll want to kill me based on a false perception. I have to worry about the negative effects on our kids. And you never asked about Julie's sweet sixteen party, which was a disaster. No one showed up. Everyone was saying her mother is a murderer. All that money was wasted, and then I had to cancel her car to pay for your legal fees and my hospital bills. If you truly want what is best for the kids, then leave them alone. They're having a very rough time right now. Eventually, you can talk to them and maybe reenter their lives, but I can't allow that right now. You need to go somewhere and make a fresh new life for yourself."

I didn't want to have to admit it, but he was right. Had the tables been turned, I would have done the same.

"And let me ask you, has it even set in your mind that you made a mistake and killed an innocent woman and an even more innocent baby?" he asked.

I sat silent as I pondered on the thought. "No," I admitted. "I try not to think about it."

"You can't sweep that under the rug. Eventually, you'll have to deal with that as well. These are the things keeping me from allowing you around our children. And if you think I just magically stopped loving you, that's not true. I still love you, but I just wish I would have let go a long time ago when the alarms were blaring. I said you were being Superwoman for everyone else, but the truth is, you were my Superwoman. I don't know how you did half of what you did and still managed a pretty lucrative career. Although I brought in a high income, I always knew it was you taking care of our family, helping us all have a good life. You handled the budgets, the kids, their activities, your family, my family, your career, and sometimes parts of my career, and you handled an unappreciative husband. Yeah, that's definitely a Superwoman."

I smiled. Why couldn't he say these things before? Maybe Brittany would still be alive. I wouldn't have felt so insecure. I just needed to know I mattered and was important in his life. But then again, had I waited just a few minutes longer, my whole life would be different and happy. Now I have nothing or no one. My only friend had to put distance between us for the sake of his business. My mother chose my evil sister over me. I have no more church home to seek counsel. My family and home are no longer mine—all gone, with the stroke of a pen.

But thankfully, I set aside some rainy day funds when I started working with Kenny. That secret account is all I have to rebuild my life.

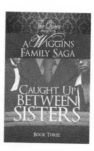

Queendom Dreams